THE
ARRIVAL
OF
MISSIVES

ALSO AVAILABLE FROM
ALIYA WHITELEY AND TITAN BOOKS

The Beauty

THE
ARRIVAL
OF
MISSIVES

ALIYA
WHITELEY

TITAN BOOKS

The Arrival of Missives
Print edition ISBN: 9781785658921
E-book edition ISBN: 9781785658938

Published by Titan Books
A division of Titan Publishing Group Ltd.
144 Southwark Street, London SE1 0UP

First Titan edition November 2018
10 9 8 7 6 5 4 3 2 1

A CIP catalogue record for this title is available from the British Library.

Printed and bound in the United States.

For Fran

I cannot sleep.

Today I overheard Mrs Barbery in the street gossiping with the other mothers. She said, 'He isn't a real man, of course, not after that injury.' I walked past and pretended not to have heard. He limps, a little, but it does not constrain his activities. Sometimes I wonder what is under his shirt and waistcoat. I imagine something other than flesh to be found there: fine swan feathers, or a clean white space. No, Mr Tiller is not what passes for a real man in these parts, and all the better for that.

My feelings for him have infused every aspect of my existence. My heart leaks love; it seeps out and gaily colours the schoolyard, the village green, the fields I walk and the books I read. My father comes back from his work at times and finds me in the armchair by the front parlour window, curled up in thoughts I could never dream to share with him. It has become a ritual with him saying, with a smile, that I have a talent for wool-gathering and that he'll sell me to the shepherds.

My mother sometimes brings me tea, creeping into the parlour as if she does not quite belong there. She bears a curious expression in these moments, perhaps best described as a mixture of pride and worry. It troubles me. I think she knows my mind, even though we have never spoken of it. She was once an uneducated version of me, of course – the raw clay from which I am formed. But then she returns to the kitchen, and there she is a different woman, bustling to and fro, laying out plates for the workers at the long oak table. The workers are the remains, and the reminder, of the war, but they work hard, as does everyone on the farm, including the animals. Apart from me. I am marked for something else.

This is a different age, a new era, and my feelings are all the finer and brighter for my luck in having the time to explore them. The upward path of humanity, out of the terrible trenches, will come from the cultivation of the mind. And women will have an important role in this, as teachers, as mentors, to the exceptional men who will grow from the smallest boys, with our guidance.

Once I asked my father if, once all the young men were dead, they would send women to fight at the front, and he said I had the mother of all imaginations. Well, that is what is needed now. After such a war people must think new thoughts, give birth to lofty emotions, and love is surely the best place to begin. I am in love. I am in love: Shirley Fearn, landowner's daughter, is filled to the brim with love for Mr Tiller.

Look how love coats me in a shiny slick that no grim thought can penetrate. It lights the dark, and distinguishes my being. I am set alight by it. Great deeds no longer belong only to Field Marshal Haig and his like – to the real men, as Mrs Barbery would have it; it is now within the province of schoolgirls and cripples to act as heroes. Greatness is, for the first time, universal.

Besides, I am not so very young, and could have left school two years ago if my father wished it. I am about to turn 17 years of age, and Mr Tiller only limps a little.

Outside my window, the owls screech and the leaves of the trees murmur and hush. I can picture the branches swaying in the breeze. The fields have been sown and the crops are growing, slowly pushing from their hidden roots. The worms and moles are there, burrowing blind, busy busy busy in the earth. Such thoughts of dampness in the dark quiet my mind, and lead me down to my sleep.

* * *

The land is green and sweet. The walk to school – a few miles from the farm to the outskirts of the village – is easy in late spring, and these are my father's fields upon which I tread. I grew up with them, and I know their rotations and their long, ploughed lines. In summer they can be headstrong, and fight my progress along their hedges with thistles, nettles and squat, tangling weeds. When winter comes they turn into a playful mess of mud, determined to swallow my boots. In such weather, by the time I reach the school I feel as if half the field has come with me; on one occasion Mr Tiller looked at me and said, 'Out!' upon my arrival, before I made a state of the flagstone floor. The others laughed when I sat outside and tried to prise the knots from my laces with frozen fingers, blushing at my own incompetence. But Mr Tiller came out to me then. He knelt by me, and helped me to cast off my boots and forget his harshness.

Undoubtedly I prefer these spring days. It's easier to dream when the mud does not drag me down.

Here is my plan: Mr Tiller and I will marry, and I will become a schoolmistress to raise the finest generation yet known to England.

Well, to be precise, that is the culmination of the plan. First I must go to Taunton and earn my teaching certificate, and I will cram all life into those years so that I can settle with ease when I am married and I return to the village. I would hate to have regrets. Bitterness in a teacher can spoil a pupil, I think.

The last field ends in a stile that intersects with the new road, and I hop down upon it and follow it onwards. It's easier walking here, but I dislike the sound my boots make on the stone. The village is over the curve of the next hill. I have friends there, other girls my age, but I have yet to find a close companion of the heart. I want to find others who dream, like me. Or perhaps I would rather that this weakening need for company would pass. I do not think mingling with lesser minds would be good for my intentions.

I crest the hill, and there is the village. It seems quiet from here but it will already be alive with tradesfolk, meeting and murmuring about their daily business. I shake out my skirts, square my shoulders, and walk down to the yard, looking neither left nor right.

The younger children are skipping, singing songs. The clock in the steeple ticks down to nine o'clock. I go inside, taking care to wipe my boots clean on the mat, and find the classroom empty, the blackboard wiped, the slates not yet set out upon the desks. Mr Tiller is late. This is not unheard of, and it does not worry me. I go into the small store room, where the rows of shelves hold chalk, beaten books, rulers, and other delights of the teaching trade. I take out the slates and start to set them out on the desks, looking at the messages children from then and now have carved into the wood. They must all leave their mark somehow upon this place, even if only their letters remain.

The clock bell strikes, and the children come in. There are 12 of us, of varying ages; I am the eldest. Our desks have been allocated according to age and ability. I sit at the back, on the left, next to the spinning globe of the world – a position of responsibility, since the younger children would spend all day with their grubby little hands upon it. Behind me is a shelf that bears the bound works of great minds that have gone before. 'If you are seeking inspiration,' Mr Tiller once told me, 'take down a book from that shelf, Miss Fearn. You have a keen mind. Let the books take your intellect to far-off places, and who knows what you may find?'

The children are noisy today, even the older ones. The blacksmith's boy, Daniel, enters with a yell, and sees my frown.

'I tripped on the step,' he says.

I take a breath and move to the front of the classroom, putting the blackboard to my back and pulling myself up straight. They pay no attention, so I clap my hands together. They find their desks and fall quiet.

I am about to speak. I am sure some words of wisdom are about to flow from me, to prove that my dream of a scholarly vocation is a worthy one. Wait – nothing is coming—

Wait—

'Mr Tiller says go home!' shouts Jeremiah Crowe, who is nothing but trouble, and the children scream. The smallest ones even start to get out of their seats.

'No, Mr Tiller does not,' says that familiar voice, the one that bolsters my faith, and he limps into the room at speed, to stand beside me. 'You are too impertinent, Crowe, as ever, and you'll stay late to clean the slates tonight. Right. Let us settle ourselves and prepare for learning about one brave adventurer, Marco Polo, and the wonders of the Orient.'

What should I do? Should I sneak back to my place as if I never tried to take his? I wait for a word from him, but nothing comes; he turns to the blackboard and picks up chalk from the wooden lip of the frame. He wears no coat today, and I watch the muscles of his back bunch together under his shirt as he writes, marking out the M, the A, the R.

'Sir,' calls the irrepressible Crowe. 'You haven't taken register, sir.'

'I thought Miss Fearn would have completed that task. Well, no matter, she can rectify the oversight now.'

I am raised high, and all the little faces turn up to me as I move to the teacher's desk as in one of my dreams. I call out the names and mark the list. We are all here. From despair to triumph in a moment – how unpredictable my life is! I finish the task and look up to find Mr Tiller smiling at me, an expression not just of pride in a student, but perhaps in a future companion? I am moved beyond delight. It is as if he too has pictured our future, and found it pleasing.

* * *

I sit in my room, listening to the men eat their supper at the kitchen table below, and compose my letter to the newly founded Municipal Teacher Training College for Women.

I write of how I am inspired to teach by my own instructor, and how I am already of use to him in the classroom. I write of my knowledge of Lamb's *Tales of Shakespeare*, of Keats, of my understanding of the parts of Chaucer that are considered suitable reading, and of how I excel at the multiplication of large numbers. I am proud of how the passion within me becomes visible on the page.

I keep writing, and find myself explaining thoughts that solidify into purpose. I explain how cultural beauty only enhances our connection to the natural world, and is only a refinement of our urges to walk among flowers, touch tree trunks, squint up at fierce sunshine: this is all true learning, too. Those from farming stock can possess as fine a brain as an Oxford scholar, if he is shown the way to use it. My handwriting falters in the excitement of elucidating such ideals, but still, it is an impressive letter in its fullness. I have stated my case.

I will post it tomorrow.

I light my candle as evening falls. The workers are loud, and merry. I will read for a while, as I listen to the hum of their conversation through my floorboards.

* * *

I post the letter and receive only a mild interrogation from Mrs Crowe at the counter.

'That's tuppence. Does your father know you're writing to colleges?' she says. She wears a white ruffled blouse with an air of superiority, but she looks swollen and pained in the way that I have noticed happens to many women in the village once they have had many babies. The two youngest Crowes, a toddler and a very little one with jam on its chin (at least I hope it is jam, and she is not raising carnivorous primitives who work at raw meat to be sated! There goes my imagination again), sit in the post office window and wave at the people who pass. The rest of the Crowes will have already departed for school, no doubt, in the cleanest clothes they could muster. I will be late myself if this conversation continues for much longer.

'At this stage I am only enquiring, Mrs Crowe,' I say. 'Exploring all possibilities.'

'Are you now?' she says as she puts the letter under the

counter. 'That schoolmaster will have a lot to answer for if he's putting grand thoughts in your head.'

'Mr Tiller has not encouraged me,' I say, and that is the truth. I know honesty shines from my face. Mrs Crowe looks confused, then smoothes her ruffles. The toddler starts to bang on the window, and as she moves to retrieve him I take the opportunity to flee.

The day passes in the ongoing company of Marco Polo. What an adventurer. How wonderful it must have been to be Polo's teacher: to encourage his ingenuity, his desire to see all, learn all, and hear about it upon his return.

'Pay attention, class,' says Mr Tiller, 'even you, Miss Fearn. I see you at the back there, daydreaming about your own visit to China one day.'

I catch his eye and say, 'No, Mr Tiller, I was not dreaming of that at all.' Let him make of it what he will. I like the confusion that springs into his eyes, and the way he tilts his head.

The hours pass slowly. I watch him for the rest of the day, feeling quite certain that I'm doing the right thing, and that he needs to know of my plans.

Finally, the school day is done. When the children are gone, I loiter, and Mr Tiller looks to me with raised eyebrows. His voice is that of a schoolmaster. 'Go along, then, Shirley.'

This is not what I want. But I find I must be given a window of opportunity to speak as a woman, not as a child. He is using his superior tone against me. I look at his hands wrapped around the worn textbook he holds. I see him tremble, and then I understand. He is trying to keep me away.

'Yes, sir,' I say, and I leave the schoolroom. I emerge into the late afternoon sunshine alone, with the children already scattered for home, or maybe to the bakery to see if Mr Clemens will part with any of his stale buns for no more than a smile.

I will soon be expected back home, but I find I cannot turn in that direction, because I have seen Mr Tiller's trembling fingers and I know I am the cause. I cannot think of anything but those fingers. The village is unaware how much has changed in the last few moments, and how much I am changing within it. I feel strong, powerful, ripe with possibility. I feel it. I walk out of the yard and turn away from the road home, walking with what I hope is the air of a girl on an errand with every right to be travelling in an unexpected direction.

I was right. There are a handful of girls and boys in the bakery. I spy them through the window, but they are too preoccupied with badgering Mr Clemens' daughter, Phyllis, to see me. Along the row of shops, I cast glances through each window in turn and only see myself, reflected. I am unremarkable, surely, from the outside. Why would anybody look twice, unless they knew me well and could see the change upon me through my white skin, lurking within?

My luck runs out at the church. The wall that runs along the graveyard is high, but not high enough; I catch sight of Daniel Redmore's golden hair, and before I can duck he has turned his head. His eyes are the brightest blue I have ever seen them, and his face is red and swollen. He is crying.

I walk on before he can decide what to say to me. I know what he's doing, anyway. He stands at his mother's grave. She was kind and good, and lost to the influenza not so very long ago, so I suppose a boy can cry for her still. There's no shame in it. Although it is different for women, I know that my mother still weeps for the children she bore after me. They were born not breathing, yet were perfectly made to the point of having hair and fingernails that she trimmed herself, and now she keeps those trimmings in a mother-of-pearl box upon the mantelpiece. They do not lie in the churchyard, as they could not be baptised, so my father buried them in the kitchen garden from boxes he made himself.

I don't weep for these lost siblings. I never knew them, even though they all have names: Thomas, Arnold, Henry, Frederick. I feel no particular sadness for them beyond the pain they have caused my mother. But I can appreciate how great a loss Daniel feels, greater still than my mother's; after all, he knew the intricacies of his own mother's spirit, and had grown within its shelter. She was a fully grown tree, her boughs curved around him. She was not simply the first sprouting of an acorn.

I hurry on, and decide that I will not tell a soul that I caught him crying. In return I have to hope that he will not mention my passing presence outside the church. This could be our unspoken pact, if he has the sense to understand it.

Past the church there is the row of cottages where the families that no longer have fathers live by the grace of the parish, squeezed into small rooms with Mrs Colson and Mrs Wells taking in washing when they can get it, and then the road curves around, the hedges spring up high, and there is a loosely pebbled lane leading off, downwards, in the direction of the river.

The trees grow over this lane, forming a darkened tunnel, and the birdsong is loud at this hour. My boots skip over the pebbles with purpose as I approach my love's cottage. His house is a little way from the village, where the old sisters Wayly once lived. They died within a day of each other, from the influenza. At the funeral the Reverend Mountcastle said he thought they never wanted to be parted from each other, but I thought of how they never served a cup of tea without a saucer, or a slice of cake without a fork, and simply considered themselves to be a matching pair for the sake of neatness.

The garden is not so neat now. Mr Tiller is not a gardener; well, why would a man grow seedlings when he can nurture souls? And I like this wild tangle that protects his door. The roses, no longer trained, do not follow the latticework, but grow out at stubborn angles from the wall to escape the shadow of the house. And the vegetable patches, one on either side of the path, have the rocky clumps, weeds and stones of a wilderness upon them. Where do these stones come from? My father's fields fill up with them throughout the year, and they must be removed come the spring. It's as if they work their way up through the earth at night.

The grasses have grown so thick around the walls of the house that I have to push them aside, but at least there are no nettles. I am able to work my way around the corner of the house and then crouch down without worrying about stings and scratches. I find a hiding place; I am ensconced amongst green leaves with the delicate fronds tickling my ears and teasing my hair. I will have to comb my hair out carefully later. Later, when I return to my room and face my father's wrath for my lateness, I will be a changed woman.

With time to waste, I must consider my plan. Do I have one? No, I am being impetuous, and this is not how I pictured it. But he would not give me the opportunity earlier and so I must make my own chance to explain my feelings to him. He cannot escape from this place; this is his last resort. Besides, I like that word – impetuous. What is the point of being young if one cannot attach the adjective 'impetuous' to it?

There are too many questions in my mind and I cannot still my thoughts. They germinate, sprout and form beanstalks that raise up into the sky. I am picturing a wedding in summer with a cornflower and sweet william posy to hold when I hear the door open, and then close.

How could I have missed his footsteps on the path? I thought I would have time to steel myself at his approach, but he is close now, so close, and already in his cottage.

I cannot breathe, but I must. I cannot. I listen for him; I am a rabbit, with tender ears quivering. Has he headed straight for his kitchen? I picture what my father does when returning from work: leaving on his boots, to my mother's disapproval, and looking in the pantry for something to eat before seating himself in a chair before the kitchen fire. I can envisage any man might act in such a fashion, although maybe Mr Tiller brings down a book from a shelf and actually does unlace his boots and place them tidily by the door, as a gentleman should.

I hear a scrape close by – the sound of a chair along the kitchen floor, perhaps? He is sitting so close to me. If I stood up now, he would see me. I would be as a vision to him, and a wild one at that, with ferns in my hair and a flush to my cheeks that is far from ethereal. I can feel my face burning with heat, although I am not ashamed. It is the excitement of the moment, but how could I persuade him of that? That I feel no embarrassment in my love? He would think me young and stupid, and possibly the instigator of a ridiculous prank, which would be unbearable.

No, I should work my way back to his front door so that I can straighten my shoulders, throw out my chest, and bang upon it with purpose.

But I cannot do that, not when I do not know what my welcome would be. I must see his face first, just a glimpse of it; I must see the man, not the teacher. Then I will be able to address the man as an equal, no matter if he tries to play the teacher with me.

I can imagine him eating methodically, possibly upon a dried apple or a wedge of cheese, with his mind on his book of Wordsworth's verse, or on the lesson for tomorrow. He will be lost in thought. He will not see if I lift my head, just a little, until I can spy him through the window. He will not see.

I shift to my knees amidst the ferns, relieving the ache in my thighs, and then inch my way upwards so my view through the window changes: the low black beams of the kitchen from which hang dusty copper pans; the top row of serving plates upon the tall dresser; an ink drawing of a robin, the eye a black watchful bead that spies me, hanging in a gilt frame from the wall. Then a crown of brown hair. I raise myself just a little more, balancing on the balls of my feet, and I see his noble face, worthy of a bust from antiquity with the severe slope to the nose but a gentle draw to the eyebrows that softens all expressions. His countenance is cast downwards, deep in private reflection. He does not eat. He sits in a pool of yellow light from the lamp beside him at the table, and he slowly unbuttons his waistcoat. Still his fingers tremble.

I am imprisoned by my love for him. I cannot look away. He is unguarded; he thinks he is alone, but I am here. I am here! I belong to him, and I cannot be freed from the glamour his slow unbuttoning casts upon me.

He opens up his waistcoat and then commences upon the studs of his shirt sleeves. Then he reaches behind his slim, long neck and removes his collar. All the studs are placed upon the table. He slumps, as if these actions have allowed relaxation to come to him. Yes, this is the man.

This is whom I wish to marry.

I should move to the door and knock, say my piece before the perfect moment is lost, but then I see his chin raise up once more, and he is about the business of his remaining buttons.

I have seen my father in his vest often enough, but it is not a vest that Mr Tiller begins to expose. It is skin.

No, it is not skin. It is the puckered edge of a thick scar, white and ridged at the hollow of his throat, leading down, and I remember what Mrs Barbery said – that he was not a real man. I am afraid of what I am about to see.

He unbuttons all the way down to the line of his trousers, pulls open the leaves of his shirt front, and then I see the scar is not a scar. It is a pattern revealed, which decorates the entire of his chest and stomach, and lower; I cannot comprehend so many lines and angles, made in his flesh. Except in the centre of the pattern, where there is no flesh at all. There is rock.

How can it be rock? It is solid, and juts forth from the bottom of his ribcage, making a mountain range in miniature, sunk into the body in places and erupting forth in others. There are seams of a bright material within it that catch the lamplight, and glitter, delicate and silvery as spider thread.

Mr Tiller places his hands upon the rock and throws back his head, his eyes closed, his mouth open. He forms words that I cannot hear; perhaps he does not speak them aloud. I am struck by the thought that he is communing with it.

He opens his eyes.

He sees me.

I am made rigid by his naked gaze. We are caught in an intimacy that panics me; I am aware of the space between us, our breaths, our open mouths, our shared shock. The burning honesty of our pounding heartbeats, separated only by glass.

He is not a real man.

I find myself on my feet, and he is moving also, pushing back the chair from the kitchen table as he rises with such speed, but I surge through the weeds, to the path, and then away: past the gate with pebbles crunching under my feet, in the direction of the river. I hear the front door bang and he calls my name, but I cannot risk turning to see if he follows. Besides, he will never catch me and I can hear the river now. I will cross the old stone bridge by the mill and loop back around the village to make my way home through the fields and I will never speak of what I have seen, never never never.

'Shirley,' calls Mr Tiller, from far away.

I start to slow.

I find myself at a trot, and then a walk. My skirts are tangled around my legs; I shake them out as I reach the bridge. Up ahead is the mill, closed up tight for the night. And it is night, now; only the last rays of the sun provide me with the means to see my feet upon the stones. I reach the centre of the bridge and look down along the length of the river.

Mr Tiller has fought a war, and he has returned from it a changed man. I did not truly understand that until this moment. Something terrible, beyond my experience, has befallen him. The shock of it is overwhelming to me. But I asked for the means to test myself, to be worthy of leading the coming generations, and I have been provided with those means. If Mr Tiller is brave enough to live with such an injury, then I will be brave enough to at least stand upright in his presence and acknowledge it.

'Shirley.'

He has come to stand at the start of the bridge, where it joins with the road. His shirt buttons are redone, although his collar and cuffs remain loose. He looks like a man once more, albeit a dishevelled one, and his expression pleads with me – it is an honest expression, the kind I have dreamed of seeing upon his features.

'Come back to the cottage,' he says.

I shake my head. It is not that I do not trust him. It is only that this seems to me to be a better place to have this conversation. He limps slowly across the bridge to stand beside me; I think his leg must be paining him after he has hurried upon it. Perhaps he is always in pain, from that heavy mass of rock within him, erupting from him. Now I know of it I can see the peaks, just visible through the material of his shirt. It is no wonder that he always keeps his waistcoat in place and buttoned.

'You should not spy on people,' he says, gravely. He leans on the stone wall, and stares into the water that runs through the archways, and onwards to the wheel of the mill.

'It was not my intention, and certainly not my usual pastime,' I say. I am pleased at my even tone. I sound cool and proper, like a lady. 'I wanted to talk to you. About a private matter.'

'May I ask what was so important that you had to stand at my window and peer inside?'

What a question. I can't begin to answer it. I find I am no longer sure that I want to speak my heart to Mr Tiller.

'Do you...' he says, and then changes the direction of the conversation abruptly, to, 'Will you speak to no one about this? I think that would be for the best.'

'No one but yourself.'

He nods. I think he understands my meaning. I cannot simply be silent forever more, because the questions I have will plague me if I am not given the opportunity to voice them.

'Shirley, there are some aspects of life that a young girl should not have to know about.'

'You were doing your duty,' I commence. 'You were fighting for King and country. You plunged into battle. There were explosions, all around. Many died. There were pieces of men everywhere, scattered, and the smell of blood, the cries of anguish, were strong. I am not a child. My imagination will tell me what you will not.' He stood tall amidst the dead and the screaming, no doubt, with determination on his handsome face, streaked with noble tears. 'You were trying to hold a position, on a beach, backed against a cliff by greater numbers, and suddenly there was a sound so loud, a boom, like the voice of the Lord, and then the rock-face itself fell down upon you, and you felt nothing but a sudden sense of peace, as if all had gone silent, and you looked down and saw the rock itself upon you, and you—'

'No, no,' he says. 'Oh no, Shirley, my dear girl, that is not what happened. Although I must say I wish your version could be true. I do wish it were true.'

'Then tell me.'

Mr Tiller puts his hand to his face, covering his eyes. I breathe out, and my concentration upon him is broken for a moment. I realise we have now passed into night proper. The sounds of the birds settling has changed into the shrill chorus of frogs by the riverbank. All is dark.

'I will walk you home,' he says. 'It's late. You may tell your father that you were aiding me in a project for the school. May Day is nearly upon us, and if the weather holds it will be a fine festival this year. Let us say I needed help with planning the dancing.'

He turns, and starts a slow walk away from me, in the direction of his cottage. 'Come on,' he calls. So we are back to commands given and accepted, and I hear confidence returning to his voice. He could almost believe his own story, of May Day and happy dancing, just as I could almost believe mine of that brave stand on a lonely beach. Of course, we are the same! I see it clearly, even in the darkness, that we are truly suited. We are creative types, linked by our irrepressible imaginations, and our minds are perfectly aligned even if our bodies bear such terrible differences.

He enters his cottage to fetch his waistcoat and a lantern, and while I wait for him to emerge my determination to be his love hardens once more to resolve.

He will not escape the goodness of my intentions this time.

Here he is, collar and cuffs buttoned, waistcoat in place. He holds aloft the lantern and we start to walk. To circumvent the village we take a less well-trodden path that leads through the woods; it will take us to the back of my father's sheep fields, which are only good for tough grasses and mutton.

The circle of light from the lantern is a strange intimacy. It makes it easier to walk closer to him, and to say, 'I am determined to be of help to you, sir.'

'You are a good girl,' he says, in guarded fashion. 'I could certainly do with assistance when it comes to May Day matters this year.'

'In all ways,' I say. 'Does it – hurt?'

He pauses, then says, in time with our footsteps, 'It does not. It is not exactly an injury, Shirley. I would be dead without it.'

'I'm afraid I don't understand.'

'You do not have to.'

'But I want to,' I say, clearly, to be sure I am taken seriously. The trees press close; how watchful the wood feels, at night. Still, I will not speak quietly. 'I want to understand. I want to be involved in every aspect of… I am bound to you, sir.

I think you know this. I will be a teacher too. I have applied to Taunton Municipal College and I mean to study for my exams.'

'That is a worthy ambition,' he says, without looking at me.

'I mean to be a teacher,' I repeat. 'With you. To come back to the village and teach with you. As your companion.'

It is not possible to be any plainer.

He keeps walking, but I can tell he has understood my meaning, and his silence is agonising. Is he shocked? Amazed? No, surely he has long been aware of my devotion to him. I thought that perhaps he might have been prepared for such an offer, even grateful for it.

But no. There is only the slow drag of his leg and my own misery. He does not want me, even as a helper, even to simply listen to the little ones practise their spellings. 'We would not have to be...' I say. I hear the plea in my own voice and hate myself for it. I will not be this desperate, pleading girl.

It occurs to me that I do not have to be.

'You are free to evaluate my offer for a time,' I say. 'But please be aware that I know my own mind and cannot be dissuaded. Just as I know of your injury, and the fact that you would prefer I keep it secret. So it seems we both want something from the other, in fact. We must hope our desires are compatible.'

The trees part, and we are suddenly at the boundary of my father's fields. The night sky is fresh after being under the cover of the trees, and the moon is large, throwing light across the stretch of grass. There are no sheep in sight; they must be gathered in a corner, in the shelter of the hedge-line, keeping each other warm in a heap. As I think of them, I realise I am growing cold, and there will be nobody to keep me warm if I do not find a way to make myself what men want. What Mr Tiller wants. What on earth does he want? I am young, and quick-minded. I have offered myself to him and he has not replied. I refuse to feel ashamed. I will discover what he wants.

He holds the lantern high as I climb over the stile, gathering up my skirts in the hope he will take the opportunity to look upon my legs, but he does not. He looks away, then passes me the lantern as he steadies himself and climbs awkwardly over the stile. Then we commence our journey across the field, and the barest black outline of my home becomes visible in the distance, with candlelight winking in the parlour window.

'My injuries were extensive,' says Mr Tiller. 'Since you wish to be treated as an adult, let us speak as adults. I am not capable of being a husband.'

'I have heard talk in the village,' I say, primly. 'I am aware of the situation in that regard.'

'Then you should ask for more from your life, Shirley. You deserve more from it.'

'Sir, it is not in your remit to tell me what I deserve.'

'I will not misuse you, miss, no matter how much you desire it,' he snaps, and I am glad; here is his temper, here is what he feels for me.

'How old are you, sir?' I ask him.

'I am 24 years of age.'

'Then why do you act like an old man already? There are not even ten years between us. In the wake of this war, how many undamaged men do you think remain? Let me decide what constitutes a real man. Maybe you are a true man in your mind, if not in body.'

He stops walking, and bends over a little at the waist, as if struggling to breathe. 'Sir?' I say. Then I realise he is not fighting for air but for control of his emotions. He is crying. I have wounded him afresh, reminded him of his own limitations instead of helping him realise how easy they would be to overcome with the right woman by his side. What can I say to aid him? 'You will always be a real man to me,' I tell him. I move to his side and put my fingers on his back, upon the silk of his waistcoat. I feel flesh, normal human flesh. I can feel the muscles tense at my touch under the sewn panel of material.

He jerks upright, and stumbles away. He does not look at me. 'There is your farm,' he says. 'Take the lantern. Go.'

'I do not need it,' I tell him. I know these fields, and my eyes have always been keen in the dark. Besides, the candle in the parlour window was no doubt lit for me. I am so cold and tired; exhaustion at this conversation has stolen over me in a moment. I could sleep forever. 'Goodnight,' I say to Mr Tiller's straight back. 'We have the May Day celebrations still to plan. Let us talk more on that tomorrow.'

I walk quickly, cutting across the field, and find the sheep all at once, gathered in a crowd, their heads tucked against each other. What strange, mindless creatures they are. I must push through them to reach the final stile before home and they push back, shoving me, putting their stink upon me, churning up the earth under their hooves. I slip down and my knee lands hard upon a large stone; it will bruise, but I pull myself up, grabbing handfuls of their woollen coats. I break free of them, and cross the stile.

I am exhausted beyond words. There is still my father to face, and now I am dirty and sore; I must not cry. I have seen wounds upon a man's body, rock embedded in flesh pulsing with silver, and I have negotiated for love like a market trader when I wanted it to be a natural, wonderful happening. I am a woman now. I must not cry at what has happened tonight, for it is the first step towards the life I want. The rock under his skin will not be strange to me for long, and I will not cry.

* * *

I see a man standing alone at the outskirts of the village. My stomach gives a jolt – but no, it is not Mr Tiller. It is not a man at all, in point of fact, but a boy. Daniel Redmore. How he has grown in form, with broad shoulders filling out his shirt. Why does he stand there? Where are his thoughts taking him this time?

I realise, as I get closer, that he is watching me. He is waiting for me. And then I remember spying his tears last night, and I have an inkling of what he wants to say.

I am not in the right humour for this conversation. My father was far from pleased with me last evening, even with the excuse of the May Day celebrations and the imaginative addition of a runaway sheep that needed returning to the fold. His face did not lose its suspicious cast, and so I rambled and made a strong lie weak. He asked me, when I finally stopped talking, if I was telling him an untruth, and I felt my cheeks blush. I pretended to be offended, but I am certain he saw through this tactic.

How I hate to lie, in any circumstance, and particularly to my parents. My father's doubts were bad enough, but my mother – my mother simply shook her head at me, and I saw in the gesture not disapproval so much as sad recognition. It put me in mind of something she once told me, when I asked why we saw so little of my remaining grandparents, her parents. She said they had not approved of my father, and so she had met him in secret, thinking she knew what was best for her. I cannot imagine them as sweethearts, sneaking clandestine moments together, and why on earth her parents would not approve of him. It's a strange tangle of a story, and it also makes me wonder if forms of love are hereditary. Her passion was conceived in secrecy, perhaps made all the stronger for it. I feel mine will be too.

But I can't dwell on my thoughts thanks to the presence of Daniel Redmore, who once poured ink on the back of my dress, and when I informed the teacher (the mummified Mr Fisk, who looked far too old to fight but went ahead anyway, and met his end at Verdun) followed me home and pushed me into a nettle patch as punishment.

'Good morning,' he says, like a gentleman greeting a lady, so he is either teasing me or he wants something.

'Good morning, Master Redmore,' I reply. Two can play this game. I do not alter my pace, but he puts out his arm and I must stop or walk into him.

'Where were you going, yesterday?'

His tears in the graveyard are the least of my concern, but they seem to be of the utmost importance to him. I find I do not want him to suffer, or consider me the kind of girl who would call him crybaby to his friends. His anxious eyes touch my heart.

'Listen,' I say. 'If you don't speak of seeing me, I won't speak of seeing you. How will that be?'

'I don't care much for you seeing me one way or the other, but I saw you.' He steps closer to me, and something about this proximity disturbs me in a way I cannot bear for long.

'Let me pass,' I tell him, attempting to find a haughty tone, but all I manage is a conspiratorial whisper. How I hate myself when I cannot control my feelings in the same way I can control my thoughts.

'Were you going to meet with him?' Daniel says.

I can hear my own breathing, and his, and I feel very afraid. I have never felt this way before; it is the devouring fear of being exposed, of having my intentions towards Mr Tiller revealed, and being made a laughing stock.

'I was thinking my own thoughts,' I say. 'Down by the river.

27

I find the bridge is a good place for quiet contemplation. I'd imagine you find the same kind of serenity in the graveyard.'

'Under the bridge, where the children hide?'

'On top of it,' I snap. 'In plain daylight. I have nothing to hide.'

'You can claim that, but I see you watch him and I see you hope for him,' says Daniel, 'and it's embarrassing to look upon.'

I have had enough. 'There is no mooning on my part, Master Redmore! Not after anyone. Not even you.' Now where did those words come from? He looks oddly pleased with himself, all of a sudden.

'It bothers me, is all,' he says. He drops his arm.

'I have my own plans,' I tell him.

'The whole village knows. A letter to Taunton. Well, good, I say. Good for you. I would wish you far away, all the way to China, as long as you don't waste yourself on that cripple.'

He has gone too far and he knows it. I draw myself up tall. 'I am sorely disappointed in you, to hear you talk of our teacher that way. You escaped the war only by a year or so, that is all. Just by the sheerest luck of your birthdate. That's the only reason you are here now, and whole, and your advantages must make you a better man than the generation before, can't you see that? Instead of sowing discord you must promote peace. It's your solemn duty.'

His lips pucker, his eyebrows crease, and he is a small boy in my eyes again, being reprimanded for his inkwell antics. It makes me feel both victorious and sad. I have banished the man who, after all, was engaged with my personal welfare.

I stomp off towards the village, and do not turn to see if he follows along behind me.

He said that it bothered him to think of me caring for Mr Tiller. Does he view me as one of his sisters, then? We have grown up together, and such ties promote close feelings.

But I find, in my disquiet, that I do not exactly view him as a brother. No, that does not describe how I feel at all.

* * *

Westerbridge is 12 miles from Taunton and 20 miles from the coast, as the crow flies. It appears in the *Domesday Book*, where it was valued at four pounds.

Apart from that written record of existence, it is a singularly uninteresting village. Nobody of note has emerged from it, or even visited it. It does not lie on the road to anywhere in particular, and is in itself no person's willing destination. Exmoor lies to the west, but not close enough to encourage the presence of those walkers and painters who seek wild natural beauty there.

Because of this, the same families have inhabited this patch of unremarkable land for so many years, occasionally marrying outside by a few miles or so (such as in the case of my own father and mother, who met through his presence in Bickbrook at a travelling fayre) but generally keeping to themselves, producing unremarkable children to suit the unremarkable nature of the village.

You can trace these families through the graveyard. Take the Redmores, as a fine example of this; Daniel's mother is far from the only Redmore to lie in the soil there. His grandparents, and their parents, and their parents before, backwards, backwards, are marked with stones. And Daniel's mother was a Barbery, and Barberys have been in this village even longer than the Redmores. They are intertwined in their histories. They do not wish to leave, or to have others find their way here to interfere with their sense of self-importance.

The Fearns are just as grounded as these others, and I am considered to be one of their number. Westerbridge, born and bred. This explains why a Redmore would think me interested in his opinion of where I go and what I do.

But the times are changing. The farm keeps getting richer as my father finds new ways to make the land profitable, and he employs more men and the ingenuity of more mechanisations to take his goods further and faster than ever before. He brings city money to this village, even if electricity has not yet arrived in our village. He may have been too old to fight, but he yet retains a young man's attitude when it comes to business dealings.

I do not think this village will be small and self-important forever, what with the changes taking place. The arrival of Mr Tiller proves that. In the months after the end of the war he came and was accepted on the grounds that a teacher was sorely needed. He was happy to take up the empty cottage of the Wayly sisters even though they had died within its walls only a month before. How neatly he fitted, so that nobody thought to question why he would choose this place above others, having no family ties here. There was also the fact that his arrival, and his injury, gave everyone a fresh topic of conversation. There is little of interest to discuss in these parts; the weather and your health can only provide so much to say that another person would willingly want to hear. So they talked about him often, and the nature of his injuries that kept him apart from those who would have been friendly, but I do not believe they did so with deliberate malice. Everyone was in agreement that a man who had been through such experiences was entitled to find his own little corner of peace.

But I have watched Mr Tiller teach the class all day and I no longer see a man at peace.

Everyone has gone home for the day, even Daniel Redmore after much shuffling of his feet and glaring at me. We are alone.

Will Mr Tiller finally look at me? All these long hours he has not looked at me. His eyes have been to every corner of the room, but not to mine. His questions about Marco Polo have been aimed at every target but me. He has sweated and stammered. Others may blame it on the surprising heat for this time of year, beating through the long arched windows of the classroom, but I do not.

'May Day, then,' says Mr Tiller, and begins to lecture me on his plans, keeping the entire length of the classroom between us. I let him speak on and on, until it finally becomes too much, even for him, and he grinds to a halt. He gets up from his desk to cross to mine and lowers himself carefully onto Mary Clissold's stool, within touching distance.

'I am truly sorry for last night,' he says.

'I wish you wouldn't be, sir.'

'Well, here is the thing. It's unfortunate that you are now involved, but maybe it is for the best. I am loath to admit it, but I am in need of assistance.'

This change of heart surprises me. 'I am certain I'll make an able teacher in the future,' I say, slowly.

'No, no. That's not what I mean. You said to me last night that I was not a real man.'

'No, I—'

He holds up a hand. 'You are right. I am only half a man. Half of me lives, still made of the flesh in which I was born, and filled with the normal thoughts and emotions of any man. You think I would not like to be married, but I must reassure you that I would like nothing more. If it was within my power to be a husband. But it would not be right, and it never could be made right, because the other half of me is not a man at all. It is a visitation from a different time, and it commands me to certain courses of action. It is with these commands that I seek out your help, if you are brave enough to give it.'

This is not at all how I imagined this conversation. I open my mouth and shut it again when no words come out.

'You don't understand, I know, I know. I don't understand myself. I try to change things for the better because of what the rock tells me, and I – I am getting ahead of myself. Why don't you ask me a question, and I will attempt to answer it? That might suit us both better, knowing the penetrative nature of your mind as I do.'

I try to collect my thoughts. There is only one question that comes to mind, and it must be asked: 'You said you would like to have been a husband if that was a possibility. Would you have liked to have been a husband... to me?'

He stares at me, and then smiles. 'Yes,' he says. 'Yes, I really would, my dear Shirley. At this moment in particular you remind me of why I would, and why I never can.'

It is enough. It will have to be enough.

'Shirley,' says Mr Tiller. 'Concentrate.'

'So how can I be of assistance?' I say. With his words he has owned me. I will be his forever more, even if he is mad and this is the form of his insanity.

He pinches his lips together, and then says, 'I receive visions, instructions from the rock, and much is at stake. I was guided to this village to shape the destiny of those within it, but I find the actions I must undertake are too difficult for me.'

'What kind of actions?'

He shakes his head. 'I cannot keep you here for the length of time it would take to explain. You must get home on time tonight to keep suspicion at bay. I have written it all down for you. It will be a terrible thing to read, but I must ask it of you, and that you will keep it safe from discovery. I rely upon you in this matter.' He reaches into his jacket pocket

ALIYA WHITELEY

and brings out an envelope, which he hands to me. I read
my name upon it. 'I do not know if this is the correct course,
but I have wrestled with my conscience and I find I must
look to the greater good, and to that end I must provide
you with some explanation. I am, first and foremost, still
your teacher, and it is my goal to elucidate, and not simply
to instruct.'

'I understand perfectly, sir,' I say, and it is true. How could
a teacher respond differently? Once more I am reminded
that we share the same goals, and the thought is reassuring.

'Yes,' he says. 'Thank you. Thank you, my dear.'

Then we briefly lay out plans for the May Day celebrations,
and I am tasked with fetching the horseshoes for the
game. I cannot see that this would qualify as an important
occupation, but I feel that delicate partnerships such as these
must begin with the reinforcement of positivity, just as one
would praise a pupil for an error-ridden piece of work in
order to establish that any future criticism builds upon a
solid base of mutual understanding.

See, I am the teacher and he is the pupil at this moment!
I cannot help but smile as we conclude our meeting, and I
head homewards. I slide the letter into my pinafore, where it
presses against my breast. The sharp corners stick me each
time I breathe, but I don't mind. I am about to make myself
indispensable, and I have his private words as proof.

* * *

It was a long supper, and my mother cast many glances my way. I think she wanted to speak of something privately, but I am glad to say the opportunity did not come. Now I am alone, in my bed, after complaining of a headache.

'Headaches, now, is it?' said my father. 'She's a real lady. Pass the smelling salts.' He said it in a joking tone, but my mother frowned at him severely. I sense some disagreement between them, thickening the air. I was surprised that when she served the bread pudding it did not curdle the cream in its jug.

Still, I have other things with which to be concerned, such as the contents of the letter.

He has written my name with such stylish ease, the ink flowing freely at the commencement to make a strong 's' that tapers into the fine loops and lines that follow. He did not refresh the ink halfway through, and the rest of my name fades until the 'y' is barely visible. Never has my name looked so beautiful.

I open the envelope, taking great care not to tear it, and feel the fine quality of the paper as I slide it free. It is a thick, long letter. The writing is small and slanting; it has a sense of urgency. If he were my pupil I would reprimand him for rushing at his work. I picture him in a fever at his kitchen table, hunched over the page by lamplight. These are the words he desperately wants me to read.

I settle back on my pillow and give myself to them. I find that I am abruptly thrust into the heart of a story. No preamble is given, no address. It is as if he has simply committed his thoughts to these pages, and I can feel his presence with me as I read. It is as if he sits behind me, his breath stirring the fine hairs on the back of my neck.

Other men, those returning to the front line, told me they did not remember receiving their injuries. Everything was a blur, one told me, and I believed him. But now I know that he lied. He lied because to admit that you remember that moment of pain and fear beyond anything you have ever known is to invite further questions. And to talk in detail of such emotions brings them back to mind with a clarity I would not have thought possible for a mere memory. When I cast my mind back to my childhood in Kent I find even the most beloved memories are not clearly defined. There is a hazy glow to my mother's face as she bends over me. I am freshly fallen from an ill-advised attempt to climb the apple tree on the common land. Keen eyes and the warmth of love, like a blanket: that is my main impression of the event.

But the German who ran to me as I struggled against the tangled nest of wire that had ensnared me – the man who picked up my own fallen gun and thrust the bayonet into my stomach, pushing down, determinedly down on the blade as if sawing wood – I see his keen face afresh every time he comes to mind. Which is so very often. I do not know why he did not simply shoot me, but I do not think he found enjoyment in the act of carving my stomach into fibrous strands that fell outwards to

entangle me further with the wire. He frowned, and I saw
lines appear around his mouth, so he was not a young
man. A hard-working man in his middle years, I would
have said; perhaps even a carpenter, which would explain
his determined approach to disassembling me. He bore
a fine moustache. To this day I cannot see a moustache
without remembering his look of dutiful concentration as
he worked upon me.

I am sorry to make this so plain. It is not, I promise
you, to elicit your sympathy (which you seem happy to
bestow upon me whether I am deserving of it or not, and
is one of the saving graces of my current existence). I
spell out in detail the nature of my injury because I wish
to make it clear to you that I should not have survived.
These were wounds beyond medical intervention, and I
should be dead. Perhaps I was dead, because I do not
remember much beyond the moustache other than a
deep blue sea, warm and still and serene, into which I
could have floated for an eternity.

And then I woke. Or rather, something woke me. My
eyelids cracked open to behold the morass of mud and
bodies that made an abandoned battlefield, alit by bright
morning sunshine, with no detail spared to me. Even if
my organs decorated the fence, my eyes still worked. And
I knew, as I raised them up to the sky, that something was
coming for me. Something beyond my comprehension.

I would swear I saw the clouds part, and those still
clinging to life around me moaned as one as the object

appeared in the parting. It was a black circle in that perfect sky at first, and then it grew in size as it fell down, down, down, silent in itself but accompanied by the chorus of suffering around me. I cannot tell you how I knew it was coming for me, and me alone, but I knew it. I could see the glint of the sun upon the silvery threads shot through it. I could make out the rough, uneven surface, the jagged bumps, and still it fell, until it filled my vision and the voices around me crescendoed in their fear and pain – and then it landed upon me.

I would say it did not hurt, but then, physical suffering is hard to recall, I find. I must have felt agony throughout this ordeal, surely? And yet I would swear I felt nothing, and I did not even experience a sensation of collision. Time did seem to stop. There was no time, not in that moment of merging: no time, no gravity, no laws of the natural world that applied. The object fell into the hole that had been made inside of me by that diligent German carpenter, and it filled me. I cried out as the tattered remains of skin and flesh that tied me to the wire were severed. The weight of the rock was immediate; I felt its coldness and heaviness, but I realised instantaneously that I was free, that I could move once more. So I did.

I pulled myself free, and I walked away.

I walked for miles, in the grip of nothing worse than a terrible thirst, through a forest without tracks or guidance. I was directionless, but nothing mattered. I did not look down at the rock I carried within me, and I did not attempt to touch it. I walked onwards until, by sheer chance, I came to a place where the forest ended and farmland began, and found there a collection of wooden buildings that must have once housed animals, but were now empty. They appeared to have been left that way for some length of time.

A small barn with a heavily slanted roof, the two sides raised up to a steepled peak like hands in prayer, had a rusted trough outside, into which rainfall had collected; I put my head inside it and drank deeply, uncaring of the metallic taste. Inside, a dusting of grey straw remained upon the floor, and I lay down and slept. I had no thoughts beyond my immediate needs. I think, perhaps, these were my last moments of true connection to my humanity, because humans are creatures of the earth, are they not? To drink, to sleep, to respond to these needs and think no further upon it – we are like the mice in the fields and the deer in the forest when we obey these instincts. I am not saying that the rock inside me has removed such demands; I must still eat, and drink, and take my nightly rest, of course! But I do not complete such actions without the knowledge that I must keep the remains of my body alive only for the sake of the rock, and what it asks of me.

I did not stay long at the barn. Only long enough to come to the realisation that the rock could not be removed. It was fused within me, rock melded into flesh with no discernible seam. I thought at first of trying to prise it from me, but when I put my hands upon it to make an effort I discovered the purpose of the rock. It bore a missive, activated only by the touch of my palms upon it. How can I explain it? The rock itself was a tool of communication, and it opened a...portal within my mind. A portal to the future.

I thought I was going mad, of course. It took me a long time to understand that the images I received were not originating from a disturbance within my own mind, but from the rock.

I cannot adequately describe what I see except in the most general of terms, for it makes no sense in words and my arm is already tired of writing. I will put this down, then, and rely upon your trust in me to guide your thoughts on this matter further: I have conversed with the leaders of the future. They are fearful. They plant images into my mind of the wars that await us and are befalling them, and they have devoted their lives to finding a way to end all such conflicts. They use the rock to reach back and enlist aid in their struggle. I am determined to do their bidding because I have been shown what will become of mankind if they do not succeed.

Now, my dear Shirley, I have enlisted you.

After reflection, I can recognise you now for what you truly are: you are a Godsend. I wonder if you have been presented to me as an instrument in much the same way that I was chosen as the instrument of the future. For, you see, I have been given a task that I simply could not find a way to undertake. But you – you with your charm

and grace and feminine ways – will make easy work of it.
And I promise you I will not ask you to do anything that
will be beyond your talents.

So start by fetching those horseshoes, my most able
pupil, and I will be forever in your debt. As will the world
and every living thing upon it.

Yours sincerely,
Your schoolmaster and ally,
Mr Arthur Tiller, Esquire.

He ends formally as if he has written his passion, his desire to communicate these events, out of himself. Yet I find myself no closer to understanding. Am I meant to take his story literally, or to treat it as some kind of parable from which I should learn? It occurs to me that this could well be a test of my loyalty, to see how blindly I am prepared to follow.

I must also consider the possibility that he is mad. I know men have returned from the war with many ailments, including those of the mind. Mr Whittle, the publican at the Three Crowns, did not speak upon his return for many weeks, although he worked on easily enough. Men can seem able and whole, but inside something important is missing. Something that prevents them from seeing the world as an ongoing aspect of war.

Or perhaps dark times do await us on the road ahead. This, as an idea, makes much sense to me. I can picture the final remains of humanity in some terrible future, reaching back in desperation to right a wrong that never should have occurred. I think many people would wish for the ability to correct mistakes already made.

Well, he calls upon my trust, and so I will prove myself. Besides, there is no decision to be made, not yet. Thinking of it in practical terms alone, I must fetch the horseshoes; this is my instruction. It's hardly a daring dash across no-man's land. I will complete my task, yet reserve my judgement. If Mr Tiller is unsound, I will try to restore him to health. If he fights a brave and true battle for humanity, I will aid him as best I can. As befits a woman in love, I will do my best for his continued good. I will be his confidante and ally. He will soon realise that he can rely upon me utterly.

I put the letter under my nightdress, against my bosom. It will not leave the proximity of my body at any time; that is the safest way. The roughness of the paper brings with it a sudden awareness of my own flesh – the perfection of it, unmarred by injury. How clean and whole I am. Is it sinful to think so? What would I do if someone took a blade to me, sliced me through? Would I fight to live on, no matter what the cost? Would I accept strange visions and the perversion of my form as the price of survival?

I blow out the candle on my bedside drawer and nestle down. I picture Mr Tiller's smile. I have never felt so close to him. And yet it is not his body that I see, but a strong, supple one. I squeeze my legs together, feeling the shame of such thoughts. In the fevered grip of my overstimulated imagination I cannot sleep. I do not even try to sleep.

* * *

Saturday morning, and I am at my task.

I have always liked the smithy, which is a place of interest and excitement for irregular visitors, although I suspect it is a hell of sweaty tedium for those who work there. There has been a Redmore's in Westerbridge for an age, working alongside the farms to provide hoes, shovels and ploughs, and shoes for the horses, of course. The Redmore men all carry heavy-set shoulders and an attitude of forbearance, as if the responsibility of the smithy is a cross they must all carry across the generations.

It occurs to me, as I find the shop door locked tight and skirt around the wall to the forge instead, that Daniel does not quite fit this pattern. Yes, he has the strong shoulders, but he is not destined for this life in the same way as his older brother, Dennis. It is Dennis who will inherit, and the whole village knows that Daniel remains in school in order to work on his talent for thinking instead. Mr Redmore – their father – has plans to expand the business, it is said, and wants Daniel's learning to make him into some sort of manager. Managers wear suits and make charts, and I am not altogether sure that this will suit Daniel. But then neither would the life of a blacksmith, and so he goes along cheerfully enough, not being one thing or another, except a general annoyance to me.

I can see the glow of the forge at the centre of the open-sided stone building, and the smell of smoke and hot iron is strong. And then there is the sound: the roar of the flames, like a monster caught in a deep pit, and I see Dennis standing at it, the strings of his heavy apron caught at his back as his muscles bunch. He is working.

'Hello there, Miss Fearn,' says a deep voice behind me, gravelly with age and experience. Mr Redmore steps forward, out of the gloom; he has been standing at the back wall of the forge the whole time, and I did not see him. 'It seems a time since I've seen you here.'

'It has been a fair while,' I say. He went away to fight, but returned unhurt. I remember I saw him in church on the Sunday after his return, but he has not attended since.

'Farm business? Or have you come to see Daniel? He's gone to Taunton to make a delivery.'

'No,' I say, quickly, and Mr Redmore moves further out, into the light, and smiles at me in a knowing way that I do not much like. 'I am on business for Mr Tiller, in point of fact.'

'Indeed? He has you running errands, has he?'

There is a tremendous noise, like a great bell ringing close by, making me start. Mr Redmore does not even flinch. He flicks one hand towards the forge; I follow the gesture with my eyes and see that Dennis has moved to the anvil and is hammering at heated metal with a patient, steady stroke, moulding it to his will. He pounds in a rhythm over which I must shout to be heard.

'For May Day. Horseshoes.'

'Of course, of course.' Mr Redmore nods. 'Do you want to take them now? They'll be heavy, though. I can get Daniel to carry them to wherever you would like when he returns. It'll be a few hours yet.'

'I can manage myself,' I say.

He raises his eyebrows, then turns away and walks back into the darkness of the building, and I can see that he has become so much older since I last saw him, stiff in his gait. Perhaps it will not be long until Dennis takes over the running of the smithy. It makes me sad to see the slow, painful tread of his feet over the well-worn floor, and the way his hair thins at the back and looks threadbare where it meets his collar.

If I could see my own parents with such objectivity, would they look so much older too? What, then, would they think of such changes in themselves? Do they hate the passage of time, or will that emotion shrivel along with their bodies?

Perhaps all old people look upon the young with envious eyes, and give their orders to reach beyond their natural time and steal from ours.

These thoughts are uncomfortable, so I put them aside in order to concentrate on my mission. Mr Redmore emerges with a wooden box in his hands that does not look too heavy. He walks past Dennis, who ceases hammering as he looks up at his father, and then sees me with a frown. Dennis is only two years older than me but he has always kept a distance, as if we are not meant to socialise. It always seems to me that he acts as if he has a secret knowledge that he imagines I could not possibly understand, even though I am the better learner by far within the confines of the classroom.

'What're you after?' he says. 'Daniel's not here. He's gone to Taunton.'

'Manners,' says Mr Redmore.

I wonder why everyone keeps telling me about Daniel. It's not as if I have done anything to encourage the belief that I have an interest in him, and I do not urge him to be interested in me. Besides, if I did want to see Daniel, it would hardly do for a young lady to turn up at a gentleman's house in the hope of catching a glimpse of him.

'Here,' says Mr Redmore, and holds out the box. It has no lid and is about the size of the bible on the lectern in our church. The horseshoes are arranged within, in two rows. I put my hands out, so he places the box in my arms and relaxes his grip a little, just so I can feel the weight of it. He laughs as I stagger, and lifts the box up. 'Told you,' he says, quite kindly, then, 'come on, lead the way, Miss Fearn, and direct me to the place for these. I'll deliver myself just this once. It will take me back to my youth when I ran the length of this village and beyond carrying all manner of whatnots. Back to the farm, is it?'

'No,' I say. I know when I have lost a battle. 'To the schoolroom, please.'

'Very well.'

I start walking, aware of Mr Redmore's presence behind me; he keeps pace to stay in my wake. What a strange procession we must be to behold, and when we reach the main street and start to spy familiar faces I find myself blushing fiercely. Why do they all smile at the sight of us, as if they are complicit in some joke? I cannot bear it, so I stop walking and turn to Mr Redmore. He is smiling too.

'Everyone is very cheerful today,' I say, as he catches up with me, and then I dawdle so that he must walk alongside me whether he likes it or not. He carries the box so easily and there is no strain in his voice as he replies.

'It being a lovely Saturday is the cause of that, I dare say.'

'Indeed. It has made them all very jolly.'

'May is a lovely month,' he says, then nods in greeting to Mrs Norman and her children, the six of them hand in hand behind her crocodile-style.

'But we are not quite in May yet.'

'No. Not quite. But it will not be long. And then it is only a month or so until your schooling days are over, is it not? Yours and Daniel's.'

'Perhaps,' I say, coolly.

'O ho!' he says, but does not comment further.

How I hate this village sometimes, and the people in it.

We reach the schoolroom, but my destination is behind it – the hut that lurks in the long grass behind what was once a cricket pitch when Mr Fisk was in charge and keen on the sport, even though nobody showed any talent for bowling. It is a small, dilapidated wooden shed into which all manner of objects have been crammed, from stumps to wickets to long-forgotten texts and broken slates. 'I have been given the key especially,' I explain when Mr Redmore gives a puzzled glance to the hut, and I produce the key from my apron pocket. It takes an effort to turn it in the lock, but eventually it succumbs and clicks open.

The door swings back to reveal the cobwebbed interior and the lines of dusty shelves filled with a tangled mess of defunct possessions that look as if they belong in a museum. Mr Redmore must be thinking a similar thought, because he steps into the hut and puts down the box of horseshoes on top of a pile of leg pads, and sighs. He says, 'Who can believe we are at the end of your schooling? You and Daniel both. It seems only yesterday you were barely as tall as my knee.'

I step back and wait for him to emerge, but he does not. He stands inside the hut, unbothered by the dust and the corpses of flies dangling from the roof by the thin strands of spiderweb. He fills the space, and something in his quiet contemplation brings an unwelcome intimacy to the moment. I find I do not want to be there.

Then he turns to look hard at me.

'Pretty little thing, aren't you? Strange to think you'll have that big farm, to run all by yourself. Your father is no doubt showing you all you need to know, though. He's a man with one eye on the future.'

I sense a warning in these words. I realise that Mr Redmore has also heard of my letter to Taunton, and that is what he speaks of: the place where the plans of the old and young do not quite meet.

'He took you along to all those farmers' balls, didn't he? The Taunton ones. But they say in the village he's stopped that now. Did you not see a young man you liked?'

'We must all make our own plans,' I say. 'Who knows what the future holds?'

He smiles, and shrugs, crossing his broad, scarred arms over his chest. So many burns have been sustained from the forge that the skin is puckered and shiny. 'I know that all businesses needs a strong pair of hands to guide the way. I have Dennis. And your father has you. Who will you have, miss?'

'Thank you for your concern, Mr Redmore, and I appreciate your kind offer, but I think I'll be looking for someone more my own age when I cast around for marriage material.'

Did I really say that? Yes, I really said that. I can't believe my own rudeness. He moves towards me, and I half-expect a clip around the ear, but Mr Redmore just laughs and walks out of the hut to stand in the long grass once more.

'Whoever makes up your marriage material will have his work cut out for him, and no mistake,' he observes as I lock the door once more. When I turn around he is already halfway across the yard, returning to the smithy, where he belongs.

It is as if, I think as I walk slowly home, a light has been switched on inside of me. It is a light that only men can see, and it attracts them, draws them close. It makes them think that I will be receptive to their glances and comments. I'm not ridiculous enough to think that their interest is all about my beauty or other talents. It is simply that I am now, in their eyes, the right age for such treatment.

I did go to one or two of the farmers' balls, at my father's insistence, and found nobody there to hold a candle to Mr Tiller. I thought this had gone unnoticed, but it seems I am transparent; everyone has a great interest in me, and the farm I will inherit.

In Mr Redmore's case, he wants Daniel to benefit. I have no doubt Daniel would do a grand job of running the farm. I'm beginning to get the feeling, when I remember the look on everyone's faces as I walked along with Mr Redmore in tow, that the entire village is already in agreement with that sentiment.

But my father is in rude health, and such decisions are years ahead. When I do inherit I will simply pay somebody (maybe even Daniel, if that is whom everyone wants in the position) to manage my affairs. I wish I could explain my thinking, which is most sensible, to everyone who smirks at me but nobody seems to really listen. Nobody but Mr Tiller.

* * *

The Sunday morning service is a regular opportunity for quiet contemplation on my part, and today is no exception. Reverend Mountcastle has a soothing voice, too soft and low to really enthuse a congregation, but with a mesmeric quality that steals my thoughts away to examination of a topic that has lodged itself in my mind.

Rocks.

The rock that has merged with Mr Tiller. I remember

the way the skin peeled back from the jagged stone, and the unnatural pulsing of silver through it, casting its glow through the kitchen.

I shudder.

My father, next to me in the back pew, nudges me with his elbow. He has hardly spoken to me since I was out late the other night. It is easy to tell that he is allowing the unspoken words to build up inside him, until they will erupt at some moment. I can guess what he will spout forth then; what I cannot know is what I will say in return. I must try to keep my newfound temper to myself. It is only a matter of time before my mouth gets me into trouble. I feel quite certain of it.

'A wise son maketh a glad father: but a foolish son is the heaviness of his mother. Treasures of wickedness profit nothing: but righteousness delivereth from death. The Lord will not suffer the soul of the righteous to famish: but he casteth away the substance of the wicked. He becometh poor that dealeth with a slack hand: but the hand of the diligent maketh rich. He that gathereth in summer is a wise son: but he that sleepeth in harvest is a son that causeth shame,' Reverend Mountcastle says, sedately.

I cast my eyes around the church. We were late today as my mother couldn't find her best hat (it was under the sink, of all places, and nobody has any clue of how it got there) and the horse, Nellie, would not hurry for anyone. So I am afforded a rare opportunity from my view at the back to look around the families of Westerbridge. It takes my mind from the parts of my anatomy that are turning numb from continuous contact with the hard wooden pew.

The Redmores are not here, of course. I wasn't expecting to see them. The Barberys take up the pew directly in front of us, with all of the children neatened and behaving, which is a surprise. The Clarkes, the Colsons, the Braddicks, the Brownlees. Mr Tiller, on the end of the Brownlees' row.

Everyone is standing; it is my mother who elbows me this time, in my other side, and holds out her hymnbook so I can see what we are about to sing. It is 'Guide Me, O Thou Great Redeemer', which has three verses. Long enough to alleviate the numbness in my lower region, anyway.

After the service we mill in the churchyard, as is the usual practice. The men talk business, even though it is a Sunday and Reverend Mountcastle will frown at them. But his severe expressions will do no good; they will only move their talk over to the village green, opposite the smithy, rather than cease entirely. The ladies follow their procession down the main street, and it is a warm, dry day so my mother and I sit on the grass with Mrs Braddick and her girls. They chat about the surprising turn of events that could lead to a best hat ending up under the sink without so much as a by-your-leave.

I watch my father talk business. He once told me that he does more trade on a Sunday than on any other day of the week, and if God hadn't wanted it that way he should not have congregated working men together on that day.

I was only little, and remember my mother saying, 'Don't put such thoughts into her head, Fred!'

Well, too late. The thought has stuck there, to be recalled forever more. Rather like Mr Tiller's rock, some thoughts land upon you with a crash and then sink in, and no power on Earth will dislodge them.

It is a good long time before my father comes over to where we sit and tells us he is going to help with finding a good tree for the maypole this year, and we are to take Nellie home ourselves. 'I'll walk back later,' he says. He seems in better spirits than I have seen for a while. He even gives me a smile.

My mother nods, looking not so happy with this turn of events, and we leave the green and return to our horse and cart outside the churchyard. Nellie has waited patiently for us without a peep, as she has been trained to do. But she is also an older horse now, and seems happy to take any instruction as long as it involves not moving very far.

My mother takes up the reins and snaps them. Nellie sighs, and commences a slow plod through the village. We pass all the familiar sights, shops, houses and faces in silence. It is not until we are halfway home, alone on the road with the hedges up high around us, that my mother reaches into her sewn pocket bag kept around her neck, and pulls out a letter, dropping it in my lap.

For one awful moment I think she has found Mr Tiller's confessional letter, but no – no, it is still safe against my chest, held in place by my dress, and the paper now lying in my lap is too thin. I feel such relief, but too soon; as I open it and scan it, I discover why my mother is so vexed.

Further to your letter – Invite you to attend a meeting on Tuesday 27th April – Possible enrolment for the coming September.

'Has Father seen it?' I ask.

'Of course,' she says. 'Did you think I would keep it from him?'

Perhaps I had hoped that, at least until she had talked to me first. But now I see that was a ridiculous fancy. 'So he disapproves?'

'He does. As you knew he would, or else why would you have kept this plot to yourself? Shirley, you break our hearts.' But I do not see a broken heart in her expression, nor in her voice. There is only a flat tone, familiar to me as one that issues orders when work must be done, raised to carry over the noise of Nellie's hooves. It is very familiar to me, this voice, but it scares me to realise that it is a disguise – one that she has worn since I was a little girl. Who knows what she really feels about me? Or about the entire world?

Maybe that is why she has always worn it.

'It was not a deliberate attempt to…' The words fail me. Hurt them? Escape from them, and from the farm? I love the farm, and I mean to take care of it. I wish I could explain this, but suddenly, in the glare of daylight with the letter in my lap, all my plans seem quite strange and miniature to me. It is as if they are pictures that I painted in a small back room without much light, and now I have carried them into the full glare of the sunshine I must admit my pictures are washed-out and weak against the full palette of reality. Such as that tone in my mother's voice.

'You mean to look after the farm,' she repeats.

'I could train as a teacher while Father still runs the farm and I am not needed, and then – later on, after I have qualified – I could do both. Run the farm, and teach.'

'I thought you clever,' says my mother. 'I thought you understood. I should have made it clear. I saw where your heart was leading you, but I thought you would not give way to it. The farm will not be yours to look after, Shirley. That is not why you have been given an education beyond what I could have dreamed of. You have been given the skills to make yourself bright and interesting to the kind of young man who can run a place like this. To help him, and to keep him.'

And so.

So she stops speaking and we continue in silence.

So my thoughts do not matter at all.

After a few more trots along the road by Nellie, as steady as ever, my mother transfers the reins to her left hand and places her right hand upon my knee. 'Your father wanted to knock sense into you.'

'A husband,' I say.

But I want a husband anyway. Did they think I never wanted to marry? How can it be that everything I want and everything they want is incompatible? I can surely find places where our plans fit together. I believe in conversation, in resolution, in peace. There can be no line drawn that cannot be crossed, and no obstacle erected that cannot be overcome. This is no different from a bloodless war, and I will not take part in a war. That is the very thing I am determined to abolish.

'Why did you think we took you to the farmers' balls?' my mother is saying. 'But you would not talk to any boy there, and you were proud and haughty. I see I should have taken you aside and counselled you then, but I wanted you to have your time of happiness. Now look what has become of it. I know who you would have, too, Shirley, and I tell you now clearly that it cannot be. You must find someone fit and strong, for farming is hard work at all times. When your father returns home tonight be meek, and make it clear to him that you understand what I have said to you.' Her hand tightens on my knee. I flinch. I do not know her at all; she seems to delight in ripping down my dreams. I would love to simply get down and run away from her and the cart and plodding Nellie. I could throw myself off if only she would let go of my knee. How can I make peace with such a creature?

'But I have not been taught to be meek, have I?' I say, stiffly. 'That is your failing, and now it must be taken out on me. Kindly remove your hand.'

She snatches back from me, but I do not get down from the cart because I feel a surge of triumph. I see now how weak she has always been; she does only what she is told.

She has failed me, and my father, by not teaching me my place; she is the reason I am not docile in acceptance of my place. And she is the reason my father is unhappy.

I will not behave for her. I will not rip up this letter.

I hold it in my hands, quite plainly to see, and we do not speak further on this journey. When we reach the farm I get down and walk away from the house, my back stiff, and she does not call after me.

* * *

My newfound joy in saying things that upset others surprises me. I suppose it is my only source of power. If I must obey, then I will do it with no good grace.

So I waited that Sunday, in the top field. I remained in view of the farm until I saw my father making his way home, and then I beat him back, running at speed, by only the merest of moments. I took great comfort in the panic on my mother's face, which gave way to relief as I dissembled all sweetness for him, and pretended I had been at home for hours.

I did nothing but sit in the top field, of course. I considered going straight to see Mr Tiller, but regardless of what my mother says I am not stupid. I know he would only have turned me away. He will not rescue me – see how well I know my love! He has no taste for the small concerns of the present world, but instead concentrates on saving the future.

Speaking of which, my next task has been meted out to me, but I must admit I do not care for it.

'Decorate the pole,' he said. 'Attach the ribbons. You can supervise.'

That is how I come to be standing here, in the rain, watching Azariah Barbery shin up the birch trunk that the men erected on the village green on Sunday.

Azariah has a white ribbon held between his teeth, and hammer and nails borrowed from the smithy in the leather belt around his waist. He is a monkey of a boy, and well suited to this task.

I do wish that, one year, the men would remember that the ribbons must be attached to the top of the pole before they erect it. But then this task has given the Barberys a purpose for many a year. Azariah has done it for the past four years, and his older brothers did it before him, all of them so light and flexible that they would really be best suited to life in a jungle.

Looking at him somehow manage to hold on with his legs while he hammers in the first nail, I remember his brothers quite clearly. Noah was the eldest, Hezekiah the next, and Obediah followed. I never spoke a word to any of them myself, being only a small, shy girl peeping at them from behind my mother's skirts if we passed in the street, or saw them in church. They always garnered a frown from Reverend Mountcastle, not because they misbehaved, but because they were integrally linked to the May Day celebrations, which is no good Christian festival. The fact that three brothers with such biblical names were cavorting with pagan spirits could hardly place them high in his affections. But now they are all dead, the brothers, and it is too sad to think on any longer.

So I tear my mind away, and look at Jeremiah Crowe instead, who is always inseparable from Azariah. He is staring up at the top of the pole with wet eyes, while Daniel Redmore stands beside him, his eyes only on me.

The hammering stops, and the end of the white ribbon flutters down to the ground. 'Throw me the next one, then,' shouts Azariah. Jeremiah, with his hands full of colourful ribbons bound into balls for the ease of throwing, obliges. He has a good arm, but Azariah misses the catch. They giggle, and Daniel stoops to retrieve it from where it has fallen on the grass.

It is pleasant to be out here on the green, in full view of The Three Crowns and the smithy, while the rest of the world works on. The other children are in school, and no doubt envious of our special task, but suspecting nothing as they learn about Polo's descriptions of the province of Karazan. The truth, now I consider it, is that this is another mission that asks nothing of me and that I would have willingly undertaken anyway. The horseshoes and the maypole – Mr Tiller wants this to be a magnificent May Day, and so do I. It is, after all, my favourite time of year in the village.

Daniel throws the yellow ribbon again and this time Azariah catches it in one hand, and begins to attach it.

'Leave it loose,' I call up to him. 'It needs to be able to move on the nail.'

'Hark at her,' says Azariah, to the other boys.

'She's practising to be May Queen,' says Jeremiah. 'As if that will ever happen.'

This is an insult, but I rise above it. The May Queen for Westerbridge is always the prettiest girl who has turned 16 years of age, and that is Phyllis Clemens this year, with golden hair and a pale speckled complexion, as if she is dusted in flour, befitting the baker's daughter. She left school a year ago, and now makes buns in the back of the shop and serves out front sometimes. We were, when we were very young, friends. But then I discovered I wanted to converse about more than proving dough, although she can talk on the subject very prettily and I have no jealousy on that score.

'I'm no Phyllis Clemens,' I tell them both, 'and that suits me, thank you very much.'

'I heard my father say to your father that Mr Tiller had been talking to Reverend Mountcastle about who would be May Queen this year,' says Daniel.

Jeremiah throws the red ribbon, and Azariah catches it. 'It's not up to him,' Azariah says.

'Do the blue one next,' I say.

'He thinks he's local now,' says Jeremiah. The boys all laugh at this.

'Weren't you stepping out with Phyllis?' Azariah says to Daniel, as he ties on the red. This is news to me. 'I heard you went under the bridge with her.'

Daniel's face reddens. 'Course not.'

'Your father wouldn't like it, I'm thinking.'

'I'm not beholden to my father,' he says. 'I'll step out with whoever I like. And I'll not be staying in this place forever either. Not for anybody's charms or on anybody's orders.' He casts an angry look my way, but what on Earth did I do? I have never heard of any of this, and am amazed to find that he dreams of a different life. I thought myself alone with such ideas in this village. I like him more at this moment than ever before.

'Well that tells you, Shirley,' says Azariah, smirking down from the top of the pole, and at that moment he loses his grip. I see in his face the realisation that he is falling, he knows it – Jeremiah calls out, time is so slow as we watch him fall, fall—

No. He hangs upside down from the pole, his arms and his brown hair dangling down, his knee bent backward and his foot caught in the red ribbon that has formed a loop, holding his weight.

We are all frozen in the moment.

Then Daniel laughs, and Jeremiah laughs, and I laugh. It is quite the funniest thing I have ever seen: Azariah Barbery, hanging off the maypole.

Our laughter dries, and I realise it sprang from relief. Everything could have been different. No more Barberys. The last son, gone, because of one moment of inattention. How different the village would have been without him, without

Barberys at all. He has been saved by no more than chance. A ribbon that looped where it might have stayed straight.

'I feel sick,' calls Azariah, and Daniel runs to fetch a ladder from the smithy, positioning it against the pole so that he can climb up and help Azariah to right himself. Daniel waits until Azariah is steady, then extricates his leg from the ribbon, and they climb down. They both lie on the grass, face up, limbs spread. Nobody speaks for a moment.

Then Azariah says, 'Can I ask a question?'

'What?' says Daniel.

'Why don't we use the ladder to tie the ribbons in the first place?'

We all start to laugh again.

'Tradition,' I say. 'A pointless tradition.'

'Still,' says Jeremiah. 'It's a fun one. Your face, Azzy, was a picture.' He bends over, puts his head between his knees, and makes a pretence of terror that strikes a nerve.

'Let's use the ladder to finish up,' says Azariah. 'Do I have to do it? Does it always have to be a Barbery?'

Daniel and I exchange glances. 'Enough tradition for one day,' says Daniel, and takes the remaining ribbons from Jeremiah's hands. He climbs the ladder, and I hold my breath as he finishes a task that never seemed so dangerous before.

When he comes down I find myself smiling at him, and he smiles back.

'Hello hello,' says Azariah, then he and Jeremiah run off laughing. They are not travelling in the direction of the school, needless to say. Ah well; perhaps they deserve a little time to themselves, and besides, I want to hear Daniel speak to me, and me alone. He looks as if he has a question to ask me, and I suspect I know what it will be.

*   *   *

Later, after class has finished for the day, I report back to Mr Tiller. He seems all ears for what was said at the maypole, but less interested in what was done. I would have revelled in a description of Azariah's fall, which is a rare piece of excitement and will spread through the village in no time at all, but Mr Tiller waves his hand at it. 'And after that?' he says.

I stand beside his desk, like a good pupil delivering facts for checking. 'Nothing else,' I say.

'The boys didn't speak further to you?'

'Azariah asked if it had to be a Barbery that climbed the pole—'

'Forget Azariah,' he says; he has had a short temper all day, and now he is venting at me. I don't deserve such treatment.

'If you have an interest in one particular person's utterings, then please enlighten me so I can oblige, sir,' I retort. I know his secret, and he must be civil to me. I am no longer his pupil alone, and I will not have him pretend otherwise.

He looks at me as if he has not really seen me for a time, then says, 'I forget how bright you are; forgive me, my dear. I must be honest with you and say that I had hoped the conversation had turned in a more personal direction, such as who will be your companion for the May Day celebrations? I've not a doubt that what I'm about to say will seem very strange to you, but on such small matters rests the fate of the world.'

He cannot really believe that. I know for certain I cannot believe it.

But I look into his eyes and I see Mr Tiller does believe it, utterly, and he is intent on having his satisfaction. It consumes him to know, and so I tell him the thing I had wanted to keep all to myself, for a while at least. 'Daniel Redmore has asked me, but I have yet to give him my answer.'

He nods, and stands, moving around his desk to stand close to me. His waistcoat buttons are done up tight, as ever, but I know about what lurks underneath the material. 'That is good news,' he says, in a hoarse voice. 'Very good news.'

I do not speak. I feel some strange emotion that I cannot place. It is a tender spot deep inside me, like a forming bruise. 'What should I do?' I whisper. His eyelids flicker. I can hear his shallow breaths, close to my ear. Yet he is not looking directly at me, but at a point above my head. If I were foolish, I think, I could mistake this for romance.

'Tell him yes, would you, Shirley?'

'Yes?'

'That you will go to the May Day celebrations with him. With Daniel Redmore.' He places a hand on my shoulder.

The bruise within me forms into an emotion I recognise. Disappointment.

He pats my shoulder, then drops his hand and steps back.

As far as he is concerned our business for today has been resolved.

But I do not want to be dismissed so easily.

'Taunton College for Women has replied to my letter enquiring about the possibility of training there,' I say, and my voice is strong, and clear. 'They wish to meet with me.'

I can see from the way he decides to start tidying the papers on his desk that he had forgotten all about my dream. My disappointment intensifies. It makes my voice and my determination harden. 'I mean to be a teacher one day. Here, with you.'

'You are certainly capable,' he agrees, and then says, 'What does your father say?'

'He forbids it.'

And my father thinks the matter is closed, because my demeanour is calculated to give him that impression. But I do not want to show a closed, humble face to the entire world! I must have someone who understands me.

'Ah, that is a shame. Attitudes can take so long to change in such places. Do not give up, I would say, but bear in mind that the time may not be right for such a bold move. If you were to defy him now it would draw unpleasant attention to this school and my teachings, and we have such important work to do before we can be free to follow our own hearts.'

'We must save mankind,' I say.

'Exactly so.'

'How do you see this future?' I ask him. 'I wonder if you could describe it to me.'

He hesitates, his fingers pushing at the wood of his desk. 'I – It is a vision, and not easily communicated…'

'What is it that speaks to you, sir? Light, or colours? What form does the future take?'

Finally, he looks at me. 'You must trust me.'

'I do, sir. And you must trust me. This is, as you say, a delicate time. Please help me to avoid a misstep simply because I do not fully comprehend the situation. Explain it to me as only you can.'

'Very well,' he says. 'But not here. I will consider how best to relate it to you. And, in return, you will accept Daniel Redmore's request, and you will continue to act as my proxy and undertake no action that might threaten our secrecy.'

'Let us shake hands on it,' I say, and hold out mine. I have a strong urge to touch his skin, as if that could help me to know him better. Is he mad? Can madness be felt through the skin, palm to palm? All I know is that his grip is soft and his skin cool, unlike my own warm, damp handshake into which my own foreboding can be read. But still, I feel better for this contact between us. Every time we speak I draw a little closer to understanding him, and reminding him that I am a woman as well as an assistant. Well, perhaps not a grown woman yet, but certainly on the way.

'Good afternoon, then,' I say, as he breaks the contact.

'Yes, hurry on home now, Miss Fearn,' he says.

So I do. I will obey the commands, for now. Everything I do will be for Mr Tiller's good, whether he understands that or not.

* * *

I will make a list, in my head.

Here is what has happened: I told Daniel Redmore that I would step out with him on May Day; I vacillated upon the subject of my upcoming interview, changing my mind first one way and then the other at least 20 times a day; and Reverend Mountcastle informed the congregation this Sunday morning that I am to be the May Queen.

Here is what hasn't happened: Mr Tiller has not attempted to explain his vision to me. I am supposing it is a very difficult thing to elucidate, but that does not excuse him in my eyes. He asks much of me, and I only ask for this illumination in return.

I sit by the stream, in the shade of the horse-chestnut tree so that I will not take on too much colour before May Day, and consider.

Perhaps, if I am very honest, I should admit to myself that Mr Tiller is not asking so very much of me. I liked the way Daniel's eyes widened when I met him on the walk to school and told him I would be his girl. I liked the looks I got from the others, young and old, as the news spread around the church that I am to be the May Queen. It is as if I have been made a hundred times prettier, and that is powerful magic. The men stand back as I leave the pew, and I feel them scanning my walk, my small smile. They define me anew. The May Queen for a day. A Queen may give orders, and expects to be obeyed.

But I will make a good and kind Queen. I will do my duty well. I will sit on the throne (a wooden chair bedecked with flowers) with aplomb and reign over the festivities, a smile on my lips and a floral crown upon my brow.

I wonder if Phyllis Clemens is very upset over this turn of events?

Father is out visiting this Sunday afternoon, enjoying himself in conversation with the other men no doubt, saying the things he will not say directly to me. And I am enjoying my afternoon, alone. It's good to be in solitude, particularly with so much to consider.

The daisies grow thick here, in the lowest part of the bottom fields where the stream flows through, and there are wild flowers springing up too, stretching for their place in the sun, finding footholds between the rocks. Are they at war, then, with each other? Do they vie for survival, much as humans do? If that is so then I cannot understand why they give me such a feeling of peace when I am amongst them. But, of course, I am not one of them. I am only an observer of their silent struggle, and could never truly understand it. For there is a great distance between us, a distance of intellect. Do flowers have their own strange thoughts? I would like to think that they do, and if they do then what other creations upon this planet also have their own intelligence?

Rocks.

I came down here not for the flowers, but for the rocks. There is a collection of large ones here, smooth and grey, placed deliberately by my grandfather to shape the journey of the stream on its way to becoming a river. Mr Tiller has a rock within him that he says speaks to him. Could this be so? I must conduct my own experiment. I edge down from the grassy bank to the place where the stones, flowers and waters meet, and I place my hands upon the largest of the rocks.

It is warm in the sun, and so very solid. It is a rock; how could it be anything but?

'Hello?' I say, experimentally.

The rock does not respond.

This is foolish, I know it, but it came to me that maybe the reason rocks have not communicated with humans before is because humans never really tried, not properly. But now a rock is embedded in Mr Tiller. Perhaps it tells him things because he is the first person to take a real interest.

Of course, there are different kinds of rock in the world, I know that. And also, now I think of it, rocks that are not of this world at all. Did Mr Tiller not say the rock fell upon him from a great height? I thought it must have been thrown into the air by a bomb blast, but perhaps it did not go up at all before it fell down.

The planets are also giant rocks. And meteors, too, and comets, I think. Rocks that travel through space, and one of them happens to fall to the Earth at the very spot where a war is being fought, at the moment where one soldier waits, wrapped in wire, to die...

'Rock,' I say, on an impulse. 'Wake up. Tell me the future.' I press hard on its surface. I can feel striations, lines, edges:

how incredible an object a rock is, now I look closely at it. How multi-hued, how interesting under my fingertips. But this rock lacks the silver strands that glittered in Mr Tiller's chest. Yes, there are many types of rock and this one does not match the one I saw that night.

I cannot find my answers here. I must rely on my love, and the answers he has promised me. It is a good thing that it is such a lovely day, and I am to be May Queen. I take off my shoes and stockings, dangle my feet into the cold, clear water of the stream, and daydream of making my appearance at the festival, with Daniel Redmore leading me to my festooned and scented throne.

* * *

I cannot wait until after school; I take the letter Mr Tiller has given me, passed inside a book on the Silk Route, and scurry along to the hut. There I sit, with my back against the door, and start to read.

The letter begins in a ridiculously formal capacity. It is as if Mr Tiller is attempting to create a separation between us, and it annoys me somewhat, but not enough to break my concentration upon his words.

Dear Miss Fearn,
Allow me to express, as your schoolmaster, my very great
admiration and my respect for your efforts in regards to
our discussed plans for the May Day celebrations. You

have been of invaluable aid to me; and yet there is still more to be done.

You asked me to make known to you certain information, and I will attempt to set out some form of explanation here, on the understanding that we do not speak directly upon such matters, and you destroy this letter, like my last, after reading.

It is, in point of fact, an impossible task that you give me. One can describe thoughts and feelings; one can document conversations or even inner revelations. My visions, however – the things that I see in my mind's eye when I place my hands upon the material that has become an integral part of myself – are none of these happenings, and thus elude me when I reach for language that might elucidate them. How does one do justice to the sunrise? And yet that is the form that my visions take: light where there was the perpetual darkness that characterises the human condition; glaring truth where once shadows (so comforting, so able to obfuscate the painful lines of reality!) fell; the pain of living in knowledge where once the sleep of the ignorant emulated death itself.

Forgive me. I shall do my best. Even when facts cannot be laid out clearly, efforts must be made for my most able pupil.

A room – that is the first thing I see. Or perhaps it is better described as a space, for I cannot tell if there are walls, or a door. White as goose feathers, shapeless, echoing and yet close and soft, giving the sense of intimacy for those who share it. Because I am not alone. There are three venerable figures standing before me, their eyes kind and welcoming, and they do not speak. They do not need to, for they simply will their thoughts into my head. They are undoubtedly human, even though they possess this strange gift of wordless communication; I feel a kinship with them that cannot be denied. They smile upon me. They are very wise. They send me the thought of welcome, and then the thought of now. This moment.

Then there are layers to the thoughts they implant, as if they have peeled an onion to reveal more inside than out, layers upon layers, going down, deeper, through time itself, reaching back from the now and also forward to the future. The perspective alters, turns on its side, and I no longer see layers but veins. Each family history is a vein in the body of the human race that will one day exist, and some veins are so very important amongst the others. Not the brightest, or richest, not even the best of us in any discernible way. It is, in part, chance; but at this level of consideration it seems chance and destiny are entwined, inextricable.

The wise ones guide me, pointing out things, showing me each vein in turn, every family being a separate journey that is only the stroke of a paintbrush upon a giant canvas, the millions of which form a perfect image of wholeness, togetherness. Then I realise that there is one tiny error within the part of the image that I am being shown – an error that contains the possibility to become a disease within time, spreading darkness over the picture until it is spoiled and dead. That error is a family line.

After that realisation, I mourned. I mourned for both the world and for my lost mind; for either I was mad, or the future was already lost simply by the existence of this family. But it came to me that I had not been given this gift of foresight to torment me. I had a choice. I could decide that madness had claimed me, or I could find a purpose within it. So I searched for a purpose. I became well versed in that image of the completion of mankind in all its glory, and at the place where it all went wrong. And I began to see how I could change that place, and save the world.

So you see, Shirley, I have no great answers for you that will make sense of what you already know.

I would wish this responsibility away in a moment if I had remained a whole man, but I am now more rock than flesh, and I feel the rock consuming more and more of me. I am hardened inside in ways you cannot begin to imagine. You will not understand this, I think, until you are much older. Then you will look back on this, on my next request, and see it in an entirely different light, and not a good one. Time changes everything, does it not?

But I must ask it of you. And you will do it, if you do it, because you are good and true, and you should remember that, always.

Does it matter if we save the world if we have lost our

souls? Mine is already lost, and so I have no fear on that
score. Your soul is an infinitely more precious commodity,
but even so I am prepared to risk it. You see, I feel the
stone in my heart; more so every day.

I have heard in the village that you have agreed to go
with Daniel Redmore to the May Day celebrations. That
is good. And now I must ask you to be a good friend to
him, and more besides. Allow him to find peace, and
contentment, and love in you. If he gazes at you with all
the ardent admiration that a young man can feel, then
let him. Cleave to him, and do not remonstrate or resist.

I stop reading. I look around the corner of the school hut,
where the children are engaged in skipping and clapping
and so forth. As I gaze upon them as if through the wrong
end of a telescope, I realise how very little they all mean
to me.

…do not remonstrate or resist. It would not be a sin to
give him comfort, Shirley. It would save us all. For it is
the Redmore line that condemns us all to a bleak future,
and Daniel is the cause. If we can change his behaviour
on May Day we will change everything for the better.

I told you this was a task only you could undertake,
and now you know why. You must make him love you,
and you must bind him to you, before he becomes the
instigator of destruction on a scale you cannot possibly
imagine.

I ask so much of you. Perhaps this task is why you were born, have you thought of that? I have seen the patterns of time spread—

'What're you reading?'

I look up into Daniel Redmore's eyes, and then I fold up the letter and slide it into my apron pocket. 'None of your business,' I tell him. 'Help me up.' I hold out my hand and he takes it and pulls me into his arms, pretending to be cheeky and charming while all the time I know this is only a pretence to get to my letter.

'I think you are my business, miss.' His arms are around me, and I like it. It is as if we are playing house, as we did when we were little. I could imagine us married, and this is how we are with each other every day, because that is what couples do. It is a game, but a good one. If only he wasn't so jealous. I know he suspects it is a letter from Mr Tiller.

'I agreed to be your business on May Day, and that is still over a week away. Now let me go; it's nearly time for the bell to ring.'

'Not yet…' he says. 'Tell me who's writing to you. You're my girl.' He sounds breathless, a little scared, as if he can't quite believe what he is doing. How could he be responsible for anything terrible, let alone the end of humanity?

I could kiss him, and he would soon forget the letter. But I do not want to kiss him in order to protect Mr Tiller, or at his bidding. The nerve of a schoolmaster to ask a pupil to – take up with another pupil, to even go so far as to defy the laws of the church… He is mad, and I should show his letters to Reverend Mountcastle.

But even as I think it, I know I won't do that. I will do things my own way.

'Shirley?' says Daniel. I hear his breathing, so fast, and his strong arms are around me still. We are frozen in the moment. He is my ally, and we both must live by rules set by our fathers, teachers, vicars. Well, no more.

'Listen,' I say. 'I have a meeting arranged for the training college in Taunton, to become a teacher. My father has forbidden me from going.'

'So the letter is from Taunton?'

I nod. Let him think so.

'You should go,' he says. 'I'll take my father's cart. We'll miss school. I'll take you there myself.'

'You are a gentleman,' I tell him, and his smile is so broad and becoming that I stand up on my tiptoes and kiss him anyway, just for myself. His mouth is harder than I expected and his lips dry; he is rigid with surprise. Then the bell rings, and he lets go of me. I run around the corner of the shed to see Mr Tiller standing there, holding the bell.

He looks upon me, and I can tell the exact moment that he sees Daniel emerging behind me. Mr Tiller's expression is a curious one. Does he approve, or disapprove? I don't think he knows himself.

That's how I know, as I make my way past him, that he is no rock. Not all the way through. Not yet.

* * *

My parents, knowing that we have reached the date of the meeting in Taunton, watch me over breakfast with intensity, but we do not speak of it. I am so meek and mild with my newfound ability to dissemble that I give them no reason to be mistrustful. If I place a foot wrong my father would lock me in my bedroom today, but he cannot play that role unless I give him cause.

I see now that this is a lesson all women must learn, and my mother is an adept. I had never noticed her performance before. She handles my father with her downcast eyes and serene expression. She skips over the obstacles he lays for her with deceptive ease, so when he complains about the stale bread she takes it away and presents a fresh loaf without a word. When he asks why she is silent, she says cheerfully of how she was just thinking of a funny thing Mrs Barbery said to her in the village, and relates a piece of tattle with such charm that my father forgets that he was looking for a fight at all.

Then she looks away and I see the pretence fall, and I know she is hiding all her thoughts and feelings in order to pander to him. He is an enormous tyrant baby to whom she will be forever bound.

But the story goes that she wanted him above all others, that she defied her own parents to have him. I can't help but despise her for this; she should have known better, even if she was in love. It seems love does not always guarantee happiness. In point of fact, my love for Mr Tiller has yet to bring me any happiness at all, and we are only in the early stages of our relationship, which hardly bodes well. If only love could be controlled; I would switch it off and pack it away for a more sensible use on a different occasion.

* * *

'Here,' says Daniel. He is as good as his word, and has taken his father's horse and cart. We meet at the place where the field adjoins the road, and I clamber over the stile, and climb up beside him. He looks so very nervous; does he see the same fears in my face?

'Let's go,' I say, breathless, and he clicks his tongue and shakes the reins, and the journey to Taunton has begun.

The great temptation upon me, immediately, is to blurt out that Mr Tiller has gone mad, but I remember that I have decided against it. It would certainly help to have a confidant in such matters, though. Instead I say, 'Thank you for this.'

'You should have your chance,' he says.

'So should we all. Have a chance at our dreams.'

He does not reply. All the lightness has gone out of him. Could we really have kissed? It seems like a moment that happened between two different people.

I think about what I observed between my mother and father this morning, and I say, 'You will not believe what I overheard in the village yesterday.' I make up some tale about the Braddicks falling out, I keep my voice sweet and clear, and slowly charm him into laughter even though it gives me no time to myself to think about what I will say in my meeting.

The miles pass. The road widens and smoothes to a well-worn path.

When we reach Taunton I see the main street, the market building, the houses, and the lines of the train tracks. It would be possible to live in Taunton and never be recognised once, I think. Or to board a train and travel to some place where nothing would be familiar – where every building blazes with electric light, and cars are as numerous as people.

I would be lost in a moment, but Daniel knows where we are, and where we must go. He clicks his tongue, and the horse travels onwards as I stare about in wonder, and imagine a future where I belong here.

* * *

'Miss Fearn, please,' says the man. He wears a suit and a blue bow tie, and has a greying beard, trimmed to the loose contours of his face and neck. He is exactly how I have always pictured venerable academics.

I stand and smooth my skirt. I wish I could have dressed more smartly; I look dowdy compared to the other girls, with their fine hats and bags, and shoes in the latest style. They must all come from good families. I pray these outward signs of wealth do not matter. Surely these men would not make judgements on such grounds. The only thing that matters about the presence of these other girls is that it reminds me how big the world is, and how much competition there is for the best opportunities.

I am shaking in my muddy boots when I follow the venerable academic into the room appointed for the meeting. There are dark wooden panels on the wall, and the floor is polished parquet, making my footsteps so loud that I wince with each step. And there are many steps to take; this is a hall, long and empty, apart from the table at the far end where the academic takes his seat, the last in a row of three. His two colleagues look much like him in attitude. They sit in their equidistant chairs, all facing me, all showing no sign of welcome or interest. I am just one of many girls to them.

I reach their table, and hesitate. What should happen next? Do I introduce myself?

The man sitting in the central position holds out a hand. I move to shake it, and he grimaces, and points instead. 'There, please.' I turn my head and see the chair to which he points. I walked right past it.

I have already established myself, without saying a word, as an idiot.

I move to the chair, and sit on the very edge, poised to flee. Daniel is outside this new building, with the horse and cart, and I could run for it, run to his arms, so he could hold me, and comfort me. Now I am aware of how many girls there are just like me, what do I have that makes me special? Perhaps it is better to be important in Westerbridge than to be an idiot in Taunton.

'Miss… Fearn, is that correct?' says the man on my left. He is bald, and his head is shaped rather like an egg, with a point to it as if his brain is a mountain. What lofty mental peaks he must climb every single day.

I nod, and try not to get distracted by such thoughts.

'We will ask you a number of questions in order to ascertain your suitability for the training course, and for work in the teaching field, which is, as you know, a great responsibility and an important role for the rebuilding of the country's youth. So let me start by asking you – what would you like to pass on to the next generation? What is there that you, in particular, can teach them?'

I can't think of anything to say.

But my mouth opens and I begin to talk, and I talk and I talk, amazed at myself, and at everything I have to say. There is so much more to tell them, and the words seem fresh and unplanned, unthought. I could talk for hours upon this subject: the future.

When I stop talking, the men stare at me, and I stare back. I cannot remember a single thing I have just said.

* * *

'It can't have gone that badly,' says Daniel.

I cannot reply. My throat is sore from so much talking.

There were so many questions. At one point the man on the right had to interrupt me in order to ask his question, and yet I still cannot remember what I said.

'I'm thinking it went well and you can't see it,' Daniel says. 'You're the best in class at questions, and the like. You're the brightest girl I know, Shirley.'

It's a long journey back to Westerbridge. By the end he has given up trying to console me. We are returned by early afternoon, to the place where we set off, and nothing there is different. The grass grows, the flowers bloom. He brings the horse to a stop next to the stile, and I hop down.

'Hey,' he calls. 'Is that it, then? Is that all I deserve, for the trouble I'll get into?'

'What would you have, then? Another kiss?' My voice is back. It's loud, with a shrill edge.

'Not in your mood. You'd bite me, I reckon.'

'So what, then?'

He looks at the reins in his hands, then ahead at the road. 'Nothing.'

'Right, then.' I hop onto the stile.

'Wait!' he calls. Can he not see I need to be alone? I want to hide in the fields until the time school ends, and then I can retreat to my bedroom to think through what will become of my life now. For if I cannot go to Taunton, what will I do? How will I become the woman I need to be?

'I'll get in trouble,' Daniel says. 'Over the horse and cart.'

'I know.'

'It doesn't matter, though. I had this idea. That you would

get in. Don't laugh at me, but I wanted you to get in and me to find a job Taunton way, and for us to... live there. In a different way. Not the way everyone has laid out for us. If you go, can I come? Can we do that?'

'Do you mean – go together?' I ask. 'In what form?' I am trying to grasp what is in his head.

He frowns. I see him reaching for the words. 'I don't know. Couldn't we just be people together, and forget everything else, forget your father and my father and the farm and the smithy, and who will own what one day? And forget Mr Tiller.' He swallows. 'What would it even matter, if we could be happy?'

'Happy together?' Why am I suddenly stuck on this one word? Just hours before I could have talked for hours, and now I am like a parrot stuck to its perch, squawking, awkward. I can't envisage this life of which he dreams. Perhaps I need him to speak of love, or marriage. I need it to have a shape.

'No, I mean, yes, but—' His mouth opens and closes. I stand on the stile, and wait.

He gives up. He shakes the reins, and the horse clatters off at speed, the cart bouncing behind it. I feel strong. I feel separate from him, and his plans. Why does he need me to lead his way to Taunton? He should be the one to lead. He is the man. If he wanted us to marry, and go to Taunton, I would think on that carefully. I might even say yes.

This seething sense of victory sings in my veins, and stings my eyes. I am crying because I have turned quickly on the stile and caught my skirt in the hedge, and now it is torn.

* * *

I wake late, and lie still. It is the first Monday of May, and I will be crowned Queen.

It is beyond me to be calm, even though this is a ridiculous piece of whimsy that I did not care for just a mere week ago. But no. No, I cannot call it whimsy now I am at the heart of it. There are deep roots to May Day, stretching back through the centuries. I find I have a taste for power in all its forms, on the rare occasions when it is allowed to me, and what is more powerful than a Queen? Particularly one who is the living embodiment of the spring, the soil, the seeds. I feel newborn as a lamb, as old as the rocks themselves.

I am taking this too seriously, I know. I do not care. I have so many tasks to perform today. It all starts with a knock on my bedroom door, and my mother's excited face (all our disagreements forgotten) as she says, 'The assistants are already here, come along, come along!'

I perform my ablutions, and then the white dress is brought in by the three girls who will assist me today. They are all younger than me, and sit on the other side of the classroom, but I know Gladys, Esme and Jill well enough to giggle with them as they help me into the dress, pinning it in places where it does not fit. Then my mother arranges my hair, loose over my shoulders, ready for the crown to be affixed.

But where is the crown? It is at the village green, waiting for me. I am placed upon Nellie, bedecked with flowers on her saddle and reins, and walked down the road with the assistants tripping along after. It is a fine day, bright and clear, and I smile as we pass the smithy, and The Three Crowns, waving at all I see. We arrive at the green, the maypole standing high in the centre, the open tents arranged around, and there is already a crowd of familiar faces even though it is still morning. This promises to be a wonderful day.

My mother helps me down from Nellie, and leads me across the green, to the side nearest the church, where my throne awaits. It is a wooden chair covered in a white sheet and strewn about with flowers, and a blanket has been placed on the ground around it for my assistants. But we cannot sit and oversee the festivities yet. First I must be crowned.

And here is Reverend Mountcastle to crown me, insistent on doing the job even though he disapproves. He steps forward as fiddle music starts up, and he is flanked by my father and Mr Redmore. The three of them observe me and nod, as if I have passed a test. But then the Reverend puts the crown – white flowers and green leaves intertwined – upon my head, and it does not matter what they think of me any more. I have been raised above them.

I step up to my throne and take my seat with all the dignity I can muster, and the crowd cheers.

The rest of the day is a series of moments like lanterns,

strung together by the endless, spinning music, fiddle and drum, and the food and drink that is constantly brought to me by so many people I know; but they present their gifts with aplomb as if currying favour. I nibble, and watch, and sway upon my throne.

The children make a good effort at the dancing, although the little ones often forget when they should be weaving out instead of in, and the patterns are more often a tangle. Still, I salute their efforts and they laugh, and bow and curtsey.

The horseshoe competition is won by my brave Daniel, and I bestow upon his forehead a kiss as his reward, to which the crowd roars. There is no time to be with him today, but there is an awareness between us, and between everyone here, that we are together. Still, I have too much to do to dote upon him. I wave him away, and he runs off with the other boys to take up the ribbons of the maypole for themselves; they grin at each other while the women sing and they dance, and the colours tangle so there is no way of knowing where one strand ends and another begins.

The evening is falling. I can see everything with a clarity that must be born of the cider I have been given. Verity Braddick has eaten five iced buns, one after the other, and the icing has stuck to her best dress. She is trying to clean it away before her mother notices. The Reverend Mountcastle is preaching at the widow Colson, his eyes casting up to heaven and then down to the front of her dress as if his faith is caught somewhere between the two. Azariah Barbery and Jeremiah Crowe are holding hands under the trestle table that holds the jam and scones. Only I can see, from my position on this throne, the way their fingers touch, pull apart, touch. Their faces look away, in different directions, watchful, while all the time their fingers touch.

I am suffused with heat. It is such a warm evening, and here is more cider, presented to me in a beautiful silver goblet with a flourish. I look up from it and look into Mr Tiller's eyes.

'For the May Queen,' he says.

I incline my head in a regal fashion, and take the goblet, while my assistants giggle. It seems that is all they are good for, and it is beginning to annoy me.

'Drink it up, then,' he says, with the schoolteacher in his voice, and I do as I am told, feeling the sharpness of the apples on my lips like a sting.

'Very good.'

He looks satisfied with me.

It occurs to me that since I am Queen, I could command him to stay, to bow, to kneel throughout the night. I wonder if he would do it. But he is too quick for me. He takes the goblet back, and holds my hand. He leans over it, and kisses my knuckles. As he straightens, I feel the cool air upon the patch where his lips touched my skin.

'My homage done, I depart,' he says. He limps away. I have missed my chance to command him.

He takes a circuitous path around the edge of the green, skirting the tables, the tents and the horseshoes. He brushes close to the lads who are playing once more, and to a couple who stand nearby. The couple seem familiar to me; the man has his arms crossed over his chest, and his back is curved a little as he stoops to listen to what the woman is saying. She is very pretty, with golden hair, but as Mr Tiller limps past she stops speaking and raises her head to look at me. The man follows her gaze, and when he frowns at me I recognise him. Daniel. He was deep in conversation with Phyllis Clemens. How handsome they looked, together.

I beckon to him.

He comes to me, moving quickly, and I see rage shining from his face, cutting through the crowd and the music, burning as strong as the stars. How he hates me, and I am afraid of him, but I hold myself tall and straight upon my throne as he approaches.

'Why do you watch Mr Tiller go like that?' Daniel demands.

'I was not watching him. I was watching you and Phyllis Clemens.'

'So what of it?' But I see his pleasure at the fact that I noticed.

This game we are playing overwhelms me. Why should he tease me so? I am in command, and by rights he should obey, and be mine, if I want it so.

'You are not a loyal subject to forget your Queen so easily,' I tell him. 'You must make amends or be punished.' These words come from some ancient place inside of me. All I must do is let go and allow this magic to cast its spell. I can see in his eyes he recognises the magic too. He leans to me, over the heads of the assistants, who are slumped, yawning. The night is growing late.

'Will you do penance?' I ask.

'What would your Majesty have?'

I shift forward in my throne and put my mouth to his ear. I whisper what I would have of him.

He straightens up. Nobody could guess from his expression what I have said. 'Very well, mistress,' he replies, and steps back. He starts across the green, and is soon out of sight.

I sit.

The music plays on.

Will I go to him? Will I go? Is everyone looking at me? Or do they dance on, forgetting all but the rhythm and the clear night sky?

I won't go. I have no need to go, except that Mr Tiller has asked it of me, and I do not need to do the bidding of a madman.

But I could go for myself. Because it is what I want. It is within my power to command love. To want it, and to take it.

I stand up, and the world does not stop and stare. I need give no excuse. My parents are not even nearby, but lost in the crowd somewhere, and I do not look for them as I step over my sleeping assistants and start to walk, finding an invisible line towards my destination.

Past the school, past the bakery, past the churchyard, the music fading into the distance, the night increasing cold upon my face, arms and shoulders. Past the row of cottages, taking the small turn down towards the river. Past Mr Tiller's house, where a lit lamp stands in the kitchen window like a signal, but my thoughts are not with him, not any more.

Down the pebbled lane, where the trees press close, and then there is the glorious, singing shock of the river, tumbling and breaking into shining slivers that bear the glow of the moon in every piece.

I reach the bridge, but do not step upon it. I slide down the river slope, my white slippers slick in the mud. Under the arch there is the hidden place, where the children sometimes go to escape watchful eyes; it is warm and dry, and feels very far away from the village.

It is very dark, but I can make out how Daniel stands tall, his arms lifted above his head, his hands on the stone curving underside of the bridge. It makes it look as if he supports the structure. I cannot make out his face. Only his outline, and the way his body is strong.

'Your Majesty,' he says. 'This is what you commanded.'

Yes, this is what I whispered to him. To meet me here, so I can listen to the frogs sing in the moonlight. But they have all fallen silent. We must have frightened them away.

'Come here, then,' Daniel says. His voice is young, filled with fear and wonder at the moment in which we find ourselves.

I shake my head.

'No?' he says. I think maybe he is smiling. I want something deeper from him, something real, but I cannot find the words to tell him so.

'You come here,' I say. My voice is just the same as his.

He drops his hands from the span of the bridge, and takes a step to me. Just one step. Then he waits.

So I take a step. Just one step. I am close enough to touch him now, so I do. I put my hands on his chest, and feel his skin through his best shirt, smooth skin, warmer than the night air around us. He breathes in, and his chest moves under my touch. He breathes out, and I feel the warmth of his exhalation upon my neck.

I move my hands to his stomach, and he holds still for me, as still as he can. Flesh. He is flesh here. A real man.

'My turn,' he whispers, and places his hands, so slowly, on either side of my waist. His hands are large and hard; he squeezes me, and I feel the strength of him through the layers of material into which I have been laced and shaped. Then he moves his hands upwards, and I feel, I feel such sensations, such possibilities that I have only imagined. It is the joy of the body, bodies together. He touches me upon the curves of my chest and then kneels to lift up my dress and stroke a path across my calves, the backs of my knees, and up, and up. He explores me, and breathes heavily, until I must pull him back to his feet and put my lips upon his face.

The rasp of the shaven hair upon his chin tickles me; it is a rough delight upon my mouth, leaving my lips swollen, and then his mouth is upon my neck, my ear. He sucks at the lobe, then takes my wrist and slips his tongue along the path of the veins, and I reach out and pull at his clothes, beyond any words. All softness is gone from us in a moment when I dare to put my hands upon his thighs. Intent replaces it, pure intent to a happening that is so close, a happening that I want, I want, but I do not know how to—

But there is instinct overriding all confusions, all coyness. His face takes on a blank intensity as he wrestles harder with the laces of my white dress; I do not want to wait while he struggles and so I still his hands with my own, and lift up my skirts.

He snorts a deep breath out, and then he is pressing himself against me, and I stumble but he bears my weight backwards to the span of the bridge, and I feel the cold stones against my back as he fumbles with his trousers, and I pull at my drawers for him until we can feel skin against skin; he is so hard, so strange, and my body will not stretch for him, but it does not matter for he rubs against my thigh, his stubble burning at my neck, and it is a battle we share, locked as opponents, urging each other onwards, linked and driving forward, grim with purpose. In this sensation I could live forever – to make him respond this way to me, and me alone. For if this is a battle I am winning; to make him move this way upon me is a victory that I feel deep inside.

There is a spurt of warmth upon my thigh, and Daniel stills. The warmth trickles down my leg, and begins to cool. Daniel moves away, and pulls down my skirts over my legs, arranging them with great care. He takes my hands in his, and holds them against his chest.

'Are you…?'

'I—' I do not know what to say.

'It's my fault,' he says, 'but I am not sorry for it. Are you?'

'It's nobody's fault,' I tell him, and am surprised to find I am still the same old Shirley, snippy with Daniel Redmore over every little thing because he once spilled ink down my back.

'I just mean that I will take the blame.'

Does there need to be blame? I suppose there must be. An inkling of what comes next seeps through me. It will soon be past midnight, and I will no longer be anyone's Queen. But still, it cannot be regretted, not yet. No matter what comes next. And I do not need a rock in my chest to tell me what that might be.

'I'll walk you home, and explain to your father,' he says. He sounds older. Yes, the outline of him has changed, just a little. His shoulders are broader, as if they carry an extra burden.

'I'd like to know what words you'll use to manage that,' I say, and the thought of him trying to explain the state of my dress, our disappearance from the green, and the lateness of the hour, is suddenly quite the funniest idea of which I have ever heard. I cannot help but laugh. The sound rolls out of me, and I cannot stop. Daniel does not join in. He shakes his head, and says, 'Sometimes I think you're mad, Shirley.' He does not say it with malice, but with some emotion that might even be admiration, and I remember all the things I like about him. Including his body. His body, and the way it feels upon mine. I stop laughing, and I touch his stomach once more. Yes, there it is again, that feeling that springs up between us. I wonder if it could ever be sated.

I do not regret a thing, and I never will. I tell him so.

We walk back together, our arms linked like children on an adventure. As we pass Mr Tiller's cottage, I see the lamp is still lit. I wonder what he does, awake at this hour, but I do not think on it for long. In fact, I hardly think on it at all.

* * *

They said I was clever.

I see now they meant that I was bookish, and suited to becoming a learned woman. A learned woman is a very different object from a wise man. I have had no experience of life; how could I see all the traps, particularly the ones that looked most like my own choices, my own happiness? Keats did not warn me, and neither did Dickens. I did not find myself within their writings.

I sit in the parlour and pour the tea. There are four cups to fill: one for my father, one for Daniel, one for my mother and one for me. I know how Daniel takes his tea now. This gathering is well on the way to becoming a usual cosy occurrence.

Father and Daniel are talking business.

'The sheep do best in the top field,' my father is saying. 'Little will grow there. Too rocky. You don't get a good price, perhaps, but at least it makes use of the ground. The future is poultry, I am thinking, all indoors. Maybe one day some sheds on that land? Electricity is not far away now, and I'll have it in everything, wait and see. Expansion and electricity.'

He's never spoken to me in such a way, and if he did so now I would not care to listen. I recognise I am not meant to be paying attention anyway. The tea poured, I return to my mother on the sofa and we continue to sew the hem alteration upon the wedding dress. It was once hers, and now it is to be mine; we have fresh lace to sew upon the neckline, too.

I thought nothing ever happened quickly in Westerbridge. Now I see I was wrong. When everyone of importance is in agreement, things can happen at an amazing speed. Barely a month has passed since May Day and the banns have been read twice already. My life has altered beyond recognition, and I am struggling to find myself within it. Where is the Shirley who found her tongue, who chased off impertinent questions and held her head high in the street? She has been swallowed up by shame.

It is not even a shame that I feel, particularly. It is in everyone else's eyes and not in mine. They all stare at the waistband of my apron and make passing remarks to my mother as I hang behind her and wait for her to finish her shopping. *What a blooming bride to be!* Mrs Crowe said the other day. Everyone thinks they know my business, of course, and paints me in the colour that suits their sordid minds.

The tea is drunk, and the day's work is considered done. Daniel and my father stand, and shake hands. They like each other very much, I think.

'Tomorrow, then,' says Daniel.

'Tomorrow,' my father agrees. 'Shirley, show him out. The evenings are getting much lighter, are they not? Why not take your lad for a walk awhile? Only a few weeks to go now until the wedding.'

'A month,' I say.

Father raises an eyebrow. 'Counting the days, she is, I see.'

His laughter follows us to the door, and I leave him behind as quickly as I can, striding into the June evening air with Daniel a few steps behind me. The view over the hill is beautiful; sunset strikes the landscape like a hammer, turning all to molten gold. It makes me realise that I really did like the smithy. I liked how Daniel belonged within it, in that place of heat and fire and strength. He still lives there for now, but after the wedding he will come to the farm. Later, one of the cottages that the shepherds once used may be mended for us; at least, that is what my father says.

Plans, and plans, and plans.

Daniel catches me up as I head for the top field at speed; I want to see the sun go down for the evening. He slips his hand around mine and says, 'You're quiet all the time, now. Are you so sad? To have left schooling behind, I mean?'

I have not been allowed to return to school since May Day. I have not seen Mr Tiller once since that night. Girls who are about to be married have other things to think about, I was told quietly by my mother. I think she meant girls who have disgraced themselves. They all fear I would be a bad influence on the others.

'Yes,' I say. 'I suppose I am sad about it.'

I was once important to the very future of mankind, according to Mr Tiller. He needed my help above all others, but now the job is done.

'It's difficult, I know it,' says Daniel. He squeezes my hand. 'I know this is not what we planned for.'

'We made no actual plans at all.'

'Once we are married, though,' he continues, 'we will not have to live the way they all say, will we? Then we can make our own rules.'

I smile at him. I am beginning to see he is just as innocent of life as I am. And this is not his fault, none of it. Truth be told, the more time I spend with him the more I appreciate that I could love him. For love is not the high ideal of beauty, of sacrifice, of noble deeds and chaste embraces that I had imagined when once I dreamed of Mr Tiller. It is a dirty business, of wanting and struggling and making do, and being each other's comfort because the world is cruel and there are few who want to do right by you with no thought of their own needs. I feel the glimmerings of that kind of love with Daniel, I think. And when he touches me I feel something altogether different. Not love, but want. I want him. If I will not get anything else from this life that I desire, why can I not have this one thing? Why can I not have Daniel to distract me?

Sometimes I think I could be his wife, and find a way to be, in some degree, happy.

'I wish we had more time before the wedding,' I tell him. 'It's all such a rush.'

'You know why,' he says. We stop walking, and I realise we have come to the spot in the top field where once, not so long ago, Mr Tiller cried and I reached out to him. I touch Daniel's back, as I once did Mr Tiller's. Daniel does not flinch. He puts his arms around me.

'I'm not with child, no matter how much everyone wishes it,' I say. I know this for certain, having grown up seeing how the animals in the field make their own babies; Daniel and I did not procreate, and besides, I have bled since that night under the bridge. But these things are impossible to speak of. I find myself blushing just to state it out loud now, in front of the man I am meant to marry.

'How are you so sure?' he says. 'It's better to be safe.'

'We didn't… I know my own body, Daniel.' He seems to know next to nothing about the workings of females, and yet my word in this matter counts no more than his. He told my father that he compromised me, and that was the end of the conversation.

'Once we're married we could move to Taunton,' he says. 'Or London. Or America. I don't care. Wherever you would like to go. I have no taste for farming.'

'China,' I say.

'Follow the trail of Marco Polo, like two proper adventurers.'

'I could still train to be a teacher,' I say.

He thinks about it, and then nods. 'Maybe,' he says. Then

he kisses me as the daylight fades and, oh, his lips are so very good against mine, and we could stay here and weave these dreams through the night.

Maybe this is my destiny.

Maybe I did save the world, and this is my reward – to be kissed, and safe, and serene, and loved within this web of possible tomorrows.

We watch the last moments of the sunset, and I try to get him to kiss me again and touch me properly, but he will not. He says after the wedding, and treats me like china, which I like and find irksome in equal measure.

'Tomorrow,' he says, 'I will have the delight of learning about crop yields with your father.' He rolls his eyes, and kisses my cheek. Then he sets off, down the field, and as he goes I feel the need for an answer building within me; I have to know if I did my job, and if this is to be my life from now on.

I need to see Mr Tiller.

So I head across the top of the field, scattering the sheep, and I find the narrow path through the woods that leads to Mr Tiller's house. I run and run.

Did I save the world?

If I did, will that be enough for me?

* * *

The lamp burns in the kitchen window. The roses have bloomed early and are now blousy, the petals falling to the doorstep, unswept. The weeds are tall around the house, crawling up and up, clinging to the cracks in the walls. Nature would swallow him whole if it could.

My knock upon the door is timid, but the hush of evening is too strong a spell for me to break. I wonder if he has heard, but yes – after a moment – the door opens, and he looks upon me with surprise.

'Miss Fearn! This is unexpected.'

'Is it?'

'Can I be of assistance?'

'I must speak with you. Most urgently.' He does not reply. 'On a matter I think you would not care to discuss upon your doorstep.'

He looks around me, over the lane and the trees. 'You are alone, then? I hardly think Mr Redmore would like it if I invited you into my home at such an hour. Come to the schoolroom tomorrow and I should be able to spare you a moment or two at lunch. You could see your former classmates; that should be gratifying for them all.'

'Please do not play the schoolmaster with me,' I tell him. I am incensed that he would even try to effect a superiority. I am seeing him with a clarity born of our time apart. 'I no longer attend your class. I think I will never set foot in the schoolroom again, and there is nothing left for you to teach me. And so our discussion must take place here and now or in the church on Sunday morning, in front of Reverend Mountcastle and the congregation. Which would you prefer?'

I have cowed him. He opens the door to me, and as I pass

inside he says, sadly, 'You have changed, Shirley.'

Why should those words wound me? But they do; I feel pierced by them. I try my hardest not to let it show upon my face. I make my way to the kitchen, where the usual lamp burns in the window. But all else is changed. The room is bare, stripped of his possessions. The mounted plate upon the wall is gone and no bright robin's eye watches over us. The table and chairs remain, but all pots and pans are gone from the dresser, and a large tea chest stands beside it instead, blankets and newspaper within, crumpled.

'Where are you going?' I ask.

'My work here is done. I'm needed elsewhere.'

'To another – family that needs fixing? To save the future? But what about the Redmores?'

'You will make a new family.'

'I do not understand,' I say.

'You did a marvellous thing on May Day evening. You changed the world.' Mr Tiller limps to the table, and strokes his hands over the wood.

'And I am supposed to take your word for it.'

'As you have about so many things, my dear. About how to form your letters, how to add numbers, how to understand the past and use it to view the future. Dickens and Marco Polo, history and geography, and now this. You once trusted me, and I cannot see why on earth I have lost that trust when I have done my utmost to be honest with you. But it is gone, and I am bereft to know that. But I cannot say I am truly surprised; I wrote to you, once, that one day you would despise me.'

'I am to stay here and be a wife, then.'

'And a mother, of course. The mother of great men, of that I have no doubt.'

I am filled with such emotions; I have never felt anger like it, never in my life, but with it is a resurgence, a memory, of the tender place Mr Tiller occupied in my affections, of the way I loved him in a way that I will never love again. My knees cannot hold me and my legs will not stop trembling. I sit upon the nearest chair and put my forehead against the tabletop. Closing my eyes, concentrating only on my breathing, I can survive this moment. I can hold back the urge to gasp at the air, like a fish pulled from the sea, for then I will be lost to reason.

'Are you unwell?' says Mr Tiller, as if from very far away, and then, 'Perhaps this is to be expected for your condition?'

So much for deep, even breaths. So much for reason.

'I am not in a condition!'

'No?' He frowns. 'But I was told in the village—'

'I do not care what you were told. I am not with child. I did nothing that could lead to the creation of a child.'

'But I instructed you—'

'You are no longer my teacher!' I slam my hands upon the table, so hard that my palms sting. I will be heard. 'And I am done with taking your words on this subject for granted. You will show me the rock, and I will speak with it.'

He stares at me. Then he says, coolly, 'What makes you think the rock will choose to speak to you?'

So now I see him clearly, even in the shadows of this emptied room. His superiority is no more than an assumed guise. He made me once believe that he really did know best.

'No more discussion,' I say. I point to the chair at the head of the table, where once I saw him sit as I peered through the window, and this twisted business began. 'There. Sit there. Unbutton your shirt.'

'Only whores command men so. Come now, Shirley, if you are so adamant you are not a fallen woman, why act like one?'

'No, I am not a whore, although you did your best to make me otherwise. I will remind you, sir, that I have private letters from you. I have kept them. These letters could make it very difficult for you to procure another teaching position in the future.'

He clenches his fists. Have I pushed him too far? He is transparent to me; I can see him weighing his options. Eventually, he decides to bargain with me.

'If I do this,' he says, 'you must destroy the letters. I want your word on it. Your solemn word. I should not have written them if I had known you to be so devious in nature.'

But I did not start that way; deviousness is learned. It has become easier and easier to lie, lately. I could kiss the bible in church and swear and not blush. Perhaps this is the greatest lesson Mr Tiller has taught me.

'Very well,' I say. 'I will do so.'

He takes off his waistcoat, and arranges it over the back of the chair. Then he sits and removes his collar stud and cufflinks, and then begins upon his buttons.

The first glimpse of the rock makes me shudder. The skin of his chest rises up around it in a pattern of scars. With the undoing of the next button comes sight of the first vein of glittering silver, and then he undoes the rest of the buttons with quick fingers and pulls back the material so I can look freely upon what was once a stomach, muscles, a man.

'Your face,' says Mr Tiller, softly. 'Did you imagine that you dreamed it?'

'I never thought that.' Not once. I have always believed what I saw. This thought gives me the strength I need to go on. 'I will touch it.'

'Very well.'

The streaks of silver catch the lamplight. It is as if his head is separate from his body. How can his mouth move, his eyes focus upon me, while he is rock within his core? It triggers revulsion in me, but I must touch it. I must have my answer.

I shift my weight to the edge of my chair, and lean across the table to him. There is the smallest of smiles on his face, and I know why. He thinks the rock will not communicate with me – and if it does not? Why, then, it is all within his head, he is mad, and I have been the biggest fool in a hundred miles or more, manipulated on the whim of a lunatic.

I stretch out, and put my hands upon the rock.

Mr Tiller sucks in a breath.

The surface is cool, the texture grainy under my palms. Here is my answer, if I can only find a way to wrest it from the—

The kitchen, the lamp, the quiet of the cottage, are gone.

Mr Tiller is gone. Everything is white; no, it is clear. It has a clarity of image, of thought, that surpasses colour. I am in a place I cannot name. It has the height and breadth of a great cathedral, and the closeness of a blanket around me. Before me at a distance I cannot evaluate are three men. They are pale, and bearded. They do not look at me with surprise, or with any discernible emotion.

All is new, utterly so, and yet it reminds me of the meeting in Taunton. In that place I had so many words to say, though none of them mattered. The men in that room made their judgements anyway.

I feel – I feel knowledge, entering my mind, seeping inside.

I am not learning, but having thoughts – thoughts that belong to the men – pushed into me. It is their vision of the future, and it is plain that they know so very much. I glimpse their own thoughts, and feel a depth and breadth of information that is astonishing, but the knowledge they are imparting to me is of a certain type of life, of time, of place. It starts with fire.

I see fire in my mind's eye. Not fire that burns within a grate, tamed by man, but an explosion of such force that it sends a pointed craft of metal up, up, up from the ground and beyond, into the sky, and then on a trajectory that leads through the great blackness of night, past stars and planets of such huge, luminous beauty, with so many spinning colours, and time and distance are incalculable until the craft arrives upon – another Earth. A planet so much like what the Bible would have us consider to be Eden itself that when dishevelled, sleepy men emerge from the craft they look about them and smile. Birds, insects, animals and plants, in such numbers, and in such strange accord. There is no death or danger here. They proclaim it their new home. Here, in fresh soil, they begin again.

Generations are made and lost; my mind cannot keep up with the spreading seeds of men upon the planet. So many intertwining strands of life form a pattern, woven and twisted, of such density and detail that I realise I did ask the impossible of Mr Tiller when I asked him to describe it to me. No sense can be made of how humanity remakes itself, over and over through birth and death. To see this pattern in its fullness would be more than I could stand, it would forever more ruin me. I try to pull back from the knowledge of its existence, but the three old men are near. I sense them behind me, and they stand firm and demand I bear witness.

And so, against my will and in fear of my sanity, I see the pattern of life upon the second Earth grow outwards and I would scream at it if I could, for it is terrifying in perfection. This was why the craft was landed there, the old men tell me in thought. This is the culmination of their plans upon a different world. It is a marvel that brings agony to my mind.

But – wait.

In time, in space, in meaning, there is a flaw. A fleck of emptiness in the woven pattern of humanity; a stitch in which the raw material is fraying. Then I spy another. And another. The frayed stitches are spreading, and the beauty is spoiling. They grow, and grow, and slowly the picture is altered. I am no longer looking at perfection. I am looking at a war.

The old men show me a terrible war, and it is beyond anything I could have imagined in scope, in sheer cruelty. Beams of bright light cut through swathes of men on second Earth, with all nature destroyed upon it; great bombs, not of metal but of disease and decay, are unleashed. They blister and burst. Everywhere the pale men fight until the beautiful pattern is obliterated. I would weep for it and never stop, if I had form in this place. At the end of time, there is no pattern left. Humanity thrives in the chaos it has created. When the war is over, billions live on without knowing how close they came to perfection.

The old men do not let me languish in that knowledge. They take me back to the former glory of the pattern, and it hangs before me like a tapestry. They offer it to me, and I realise I can control it with my thoughts. I can move within the generations, the strands, and pick out those early flaws one by one, to examine them in detail. Each and every flaw that spreads starts with one union. One coupling which creates one family line that grows. Just one union that creates the children that kill the beautiful future.

As I concentrate, another layer is added: a map of Earth, my Earth, laid over the pattern at the point of the first flaws. I recognise my country, my county, my village. Here is a union that chills me with recognition.

Redmore.

Daniel Redmore and Phyllis Clemens, at the beginning

of May 1920, combine their strands to form another – a strand that winds its path along to a descendant who will eventually board a craft, and beget more children upon a second Earth. Children who will dissent from the project to create perfection, and will instigate a terrible war.

But the time for that union has passed.

Have I helped to save the pattern? Have I prevented a war?

The vision of the map and the pattern fades, and I return to the white room. The three old, pale men stand before me. They have one last thing that they wish me to understand.

Rocks.

They open their hands to me, and I see upon their palms small rocks, streaked with silver thread into which they have woven their message. The rocks rise from their grasp and levitate above them; they contain so much information: trajectory, the power to embed within human flesh, to heal and to keep alive for many decades, so that the cry for help is inescapable. The rocks are not natural, but a creation of these men, disguised and then impregnated with their desperate plea to end the war before it can ever begin.

As I watch, the rocks are thrown by an invisible force, so fast that they speed through space and escape time itself, to land all over the world in different countries and different eras. The old men cannot go back in time, but the rocks can.

And the men are done. Everything is explained, and now it is my task to help them.

But I have questions, many questions, that I cannot ask. I have no mouth in this place with which to speak. I try thinking hard, shouting within my head:

If that is the future of second Earth, what becomes of my planet?

Why did you leave so many of us behind? Who chose who would stay and who would go upon the metal craft?

And this is the question I must have answered above all others:

How can I understand all of these things when you only give me the information you choose to share?

They tell me nothing further. They close their eyes, and lower their heads, and the meeting is over.

That is when I realise I am not in a meeting. I am witnessing a recording. This is a missive, a letter that reads itself whenever Mr Tiller's rock is touched. The old men are not in a conversation with me. They decide long into the future what is important, and expect me to be content with that.

But I am not. And I must find my answers within the scraps of knowledge they are throwing to me. Mr Tiller wrote in his own letters that he could control the vision, at least to the extent of repeating the parts of the pattern that he desired to see. I concentrate hard, asking over and over, and yes – here is the metal craft once more, before me. Here are those who board the craft.

I watch them enter the body of the huge metal bullet that will explode into the stars and carry them away; there is no indication as to why they are leaving, or what they are leaving behind.

My only clue lies in the fact that they have one thing in

common. They are all pale old men.

I watch it again.

Yes, they are all pale old men, white-haired. Is it just the nature of the image? I cannot tell. Perhaps it is a representation of the event, for how can there be no people of China, or the East Indies? No youths? No women, no women at all? How is that possible?

I move forward in time, to the arrival upon second Earth, and then the patterns thicken with brand new strands, like an injection of life. So many births – births of women, upon that pristine soil. But not births of a kind I recognise, amounting from the intertwining of two strands. These women come from nowhere.

The pale old men did not take women on their journey. When they reached their destination they made them.

Everyone who did not belong to their kind was left behind. To face what, I cannot tell, for this recording will not show me.

How can the final pattern be so beautiful when it discards so many threads? But, of course, nature is not beautiful. It is not meant to form a pattern woven to perfection. I think of the battles I see every day around me: spider and flies, foxes and rabbits. The land and the sea, the night and the day, the old and the young. I think of how it was under the bridge, with Daniel, when we pitched our bodies against each other in an age-old struggle in which we were born to fight. It was not beautiful, but it was glorious. And there was never meant to be a victor.

This is the truth of our Earth.

I pull my mind away. I have seen all I need to see. The vision dissipates, and the emptied kitchen returns to my view. I cannot tell how much time has passed, but the lamp burns on, and my hands are still upon the rock. Mr Tiller's arms are around me; he has moved closer, and he is tender in the way he holds me upright, for I realise I am not supporting my own weight. I pull myself up, and away from him.

'So now you see,' he says. 'My dear girl, now you see. They showed you.'

He is not mad. He is brave, and determined. He is utterly mistaken in his loyalty. He has taken the vision as undisputed knowledge rather than a point of view. He does not see that this future is not his fight.

'You are leaving to find others,' I say. 'Is that not true? You mean to find the other families that mar the pattern, and stamp them out.'

'You know I must.' He buttons his shirt, and covers the rock from my sight.

'No. No. You must not. And I cannot marry Daniel.'

In all of our time spent together, I do not think I have ever said anything that surprised him as much. 'But it is arranged. The future is not safe until it is done. What if Master Redmore returns to Miss Clemens with his broken heart, and she comforts him? We cannot guarantee the situation.'

'It is not my duty to safeguard the vision within that rock,' I state. I know it, completely, deep within myself. This is not my fight.

'It is everyone's duty! Including yours. That is why I – why you will marry Daniel Redmore and I will go forth into the world to stop others. Did you not see the pattern? Did you not see the perfection of it?'

How can I begin to explain it? We have shared the same vision, and yet will never come to the same conclusion. We stand on opposite sides.

'You must not,' I repeat. 'The future is not meant to be the way it is presented here. Can't you see it is not real?'

I have chosen the wrong word. I know it as soon as it leaves my lips. All tenderness, all confusion is gone from him in a moment. He pushes back his chair, the legs scraping along the floor with a squeal, and stands tall. 'Ha! Well, then it suits me, does it not? As I am not a real man, according to the world. I am part of the rock now, and it is part of me, and I will do as it asks of me.'

'It asks nothing of you! It does not speak of this world, or your responsibility.'

He hesitates. 'It shows humanity,' he says.

'One part of it. One part, one group, with a message that has truth only to those who choose to believe it.'

'It spoke of beauty. I taught you Keats, Shirley Fearn. Trust in Keats if you will not trust in me.'

Keats, Mr Tiller, my father, the men at Taunton, the men on that other Earth: my head swims with them all. None of them can be reasoned with. Not a one, and I want nothing more to do with them. 'I will not trust any of you,' I tell him. 'And you must not continue with this task, no more than I will marry Daniel Redmore.'

'Then you are of no further use to me,' he says, and passes a hand across his eyes. I sit in the silence and wait. I do not know how this conversation will end; I cannot simply leave, and yet there is no way to resolve this impasse. I once believed that there was a way to find peace no matter what the cause of the war, but now I understand. In some circumstances there simply is no middle ground. There is no place where two people may meet.

'I think perhaps—' I begin.

Mr Tiller springs toward me at speed; I expel a breath from my lungs in surprise and then he is upon me, leaning over me. I feel a cruel pain at the back of my head, and my hair is tugged so that my head is thrown backwards. He has my hair; he has me in his grasp, my hair in his fist, and then his other hand is on my neck, and he squeezes. There is no more time for thought. My body reacts. I kick out, and punch, and fight for my breath, for my life.

'Be still,' he demands. 'Be still, before I hurt you.'

The words, not the command, surprise me to obeisance. Does he not consider he is hurting me already?

'There now. I want your complete attention. You must do as you are told, Miss Fearn, and you are told to marry Mr Redmore. Is that so terrible? I know you enjoy his attention. It is obvious to the entire village how much you beg for it. Why would you fight that which comes naturally to you?'

I cannot look at his eyes, I cannot bear it. He is so close to me, and he looks at me with a dispassionate objectivity that reduces me to less than human. It is so wrong for him to be this close to me, and to have no love, no care, no sense of my humanity within him. He is a rock, indeed. He is so hard, and without empathy for the fact that I live, I breathe. I need to breathe.

'If you are disobedient then I will have to find another, more drastic, way to ensure that Mr Redmore's line does not come to pass. Do you understand me?'

He relaxes his grip upon my neck. As if freed from the pressure, I feel water well up in my eyes. There is a terrible sense of shame that overwhelms me for these tears, more so than I ever felt about Daniel's embrace. Shame – for being touched by Mr Tiller, for the way he looks at me as I cry.

'You will burn the letters I wrote to you in good faith,' he says, as he moves away. 'And you will do as we have discussed.' He limps back to the tea chest beside the dresser, and places one hand upon the newspaper within, crumpling it further.

I must find an advantage, I must not be destroyed. 'Will you stay until the wedding, sir?' I ask him. 'I would – prefer it. As you are the reason for it.'

He tilts his head, and considers the request. 'Very well.'

I manage to stand and take small steps to the door, although my legs tremble, and I cannot imagine how I will get home upon them. He follows me to the door and it comes to me that we have told each other lies, and become equals in that regard. Yes, he is not my master, and now I am free to hate him. I hate him very much, for the way he imagines this world and my place within it to be, and for the way he wants to make the next world.

'Goodnight,' he says. 'I hope I haven't unduly surprised you. Just think on what you have seen, and I am certain you will come to see the need for forthright action.'

'Goodnight,' I say, and I walk down the path, slowly, and with care. Then I put one foot in front of the other for what seems like hours. No, more than hours – a universe of time. An entire universe of time.

*　*　*

Imagine losing a war.

Imagine the fear you feel as it seems all you believe in will be lost forever.

Imagine reaching the point where there are no further allies to find, and so, in desperation, you write a message and place it within a bottle and throw it into the ocean. You hope and pray it will reach somebody who will feel the same as you, and who will find a way to aid you across that great expanse of ocean. That maybe they will save you. You pour all your persuasion into that message, and you cast it adrift; you have no inkling as to what kind of person might find it. You can only hope that it is picked up by somebody who shares your beliefs. Perhaps, if you send many such messages, some will wash up on fertile soil.

This is what I imagine, as I sit on my bed and attempt to compose a letter to Daniel. I have received such a message, and I will not let it sow its seeds within me. I will not be a foot soldier for pale old men, no matter where they live or what pretty patterns they weave.

My neck is sore but unbruised, I think; my limbs still quake with fear. But I will write this letter before I climb into my bed tonight. The farm is quiet and my room is as warm and safe as ever it has been; if I cannot write down these things here and now, then I will never do it.

My dearest Daniel

I cannot marry you.

I could provide you with a number of reasons, and I will do so if you wish. It will probably make this easier, because every one of them will give you leave to think me mad. I would prefer it if you decide that you, also, do not want to marry a girl who could be so changeable in nature. We were not meant to be together; will that do?

I suppose it will not, and you will want to draw this out, and meet face to face, and I will oblige. It will not change the outcome.

I would have liked to have gone to Taunton and taken you with me. I would have searched for a way to be together that came without all the usual words. I am sorry that I was cruel to you, on the day of the interview, when I stood upon the stile; for it was cruelty to wilfully misunderstand you at that moment. I hope you appreciate that I am not deliberately being cruel now.

I have one favour to ask of you: do not come to the wedding rehearsal on Sunday afternoon, or speak of

this matter to anyone before that time. I would like the opportunity to explain all myself to our parents, in the church, at that appointed time. It would be easier if you were not there to hear my words.
   Your friend forever,
   Miss Shirley Fearn

I put away the pen and ink, and seal the letter in an envelope. It is all I can do. I will hand it to him tomorrow morning, when I go into the village to fetch the bread. And then what?
Sunday afternoon awaits.

*　*　*

Not all plans run smoothly.

I would have liked my own company for this task, but my mother decides to come with me, and so we take a slow walk into the village while she grasps the opportunity to talk to me about wedding arrangements: the flowers, the cake, the chimney sweep who will come in the morning, the silver sixpence that must be placed in my shoe. She is working so hard to ward off a disaster that has already happened.

We collect the bread from the bakery, served by a sullen Phyllis, and as we step outside I tell my mother that I have a letter to deliver to Daniel. She raises her eyebrows, but does not comment.

We walk past the school. It is Saturday, and all is quiet within. I wonder what Mr Tiller has taught the children this

117

past week, and whether they have taken every word as truth. Once I thought that a bitter teacher spoils a pupil; I wonder now if it there is not an innate bitterness at the heart of education, which always comes with hidden meanings and a high cost.

We reach the village green, and my mother waits by the maypole, which has not yet been taken down, as I make my way into the smithy's yard. Mr Redmore and Dennis are at work together – one holds a large piece of metal still in tongs while the other hammers it flat upon the anvil – and they look up in unison as I call out a hesitant greeting in between ringing blows.

'He's at market,' calls Dennis. 'Saturday is Taunton day, you know that. Have you lost your brains in the rush to get to the altar?'

Mr Redmore puts down the tongs, wipes his hands upon his stiff leather apron, and then cuffs Dennis around the back of the head, which makes me smile. Of course, Daniel is not here, how could I have forgotten? So much has happened that even the simplest of facts is passing me by. I am disgusted with the relief I feel as I hand over the letter to Mr Redmore. I do not have to see Daniel at this moment, and I do not have to explain to him why I need to record in a letter that which I cannot bear to say in words.

'Would you see Daniel gets this, please, Mr Redmore? It is very important.'

His old eyes flash surprise as he replies, 'Very well, that I can do. Are you well, miss?'

'Yes thank you,' I say.

'Only you look a little wearied, but then, perhaps brides-to-be do. I remember when I got married—' He shrugs. 'Well, enough of that. I must get back to the work in hand.'

I picture him as a young man, in the days approaching the saying of his vows; he has quite the kindest expression I have ever seen. It occurs to me that he has only ever wanted his sons to be happy, and that he wants me to be happy too. I take his hand in mine, and squeeze it.

'Thank you so very much,' I say.

Then I walk away before either one of us can say more.

All depends on keeping the breaking of the engagement as a secret, but my mother takes one look at my face as I meet her on the green and reads everything there.

'Oh, you foolish girl,' she says. 'Foolish, foolish. Quick, go back and retrieve the letter and rip it into pieces, before it's too late.'

I shake my head. I am expecting such rage from her, but instead she puts a hand on my shoulder, and says, 'Why, Shirley?'

'It is too complicated...'

She sighs. I have a sudden feeling that she has been expecting this all along. 'Come. Let's get home.'

We start the walk out of the village, back up the hill that leads to the farm. There are so many things she could say and I am so grateful that she decides to say none of them. I already know my father will be apoplectic. I already know that everyone will laugh, and point, and consider me used and discarded, good for nothing any more. I do not need her to tell me.

Instead she says, 'When I was a little younger than you I met your father at a fayre. He bought me a baked potato without even asking first; he was bold, and bright, and he had a reputation back then – the kind of reputation that does a girl no good and a man no harm at all. He had got a girl into trouble in his own village, was the word, and then had refused to marry her, although nobody could produce the name of this girl when I asked for details. Perhaps it was all a lie. I didn't really care, anyway. My parents forbade it so I sneaked from the house to see him, and got caught, of course, being quite useless at such acts. He agreed to marry me, though, which surprised everyone. It did not seem to matter whether I agreed to marry him.'

She does not say more.

We cross the stile and walk up the edge of the lower field together. How calm she is; how different to what I was expecting.

'Thank you,' I say, although I cannot exactly explain for what.

'I wanted you to be better, to be beyond all this.' She gestures at the ground, the sky. 'But the more you learned, the further you got away from me, until I could not recognise myself in you. I have been so lonely, watching you make your plans from such a distance, with your head in the clouds. And I became bitter as you excluded me. I could not understand it. But this act – this I understand.'

She takes my hand, and squeezes it.

'How can that be so? I do not understand it myself.'

'What will you do?'

There is no answer to give her.

'You cannot go to Taunton,' she says. 'Put that out of your mind.'

'I no longer want to be a teacher.'

'Good, because they did not want you. A letter came days ago. They wrote that you did not have the correct attitude for a schoolmistress. I destroyed it before your father could read it, and take pleasure in it.'

They do not want me. They do not want me; well, I hold fast to my thoughts. I do not want them. No more rooms of quiet, seated, suppressed children. No more thoughts that I do not form myself.

'I admire you,' my mother says. We continue to walk to the farm; where else would we go? 'I wish I had your courage. I have long admired it from afar. I will help, as I can, to find a path for you through life.'

Honesty compels me to say, 'Perhaps you should not formulate such thoughts until you discover what I have said in the letter to Daniel.'

She nods. 'Very well. When will you tell your father?'

'Tomorrow afternoon. At the rehearsal. Do not come. Make an excuse, I beg of you. You will find out all later.'

'It will all come out in the wash, and then we can decide what to do. There will be happiness, eventually. I do not doubt it.'

She pulls me into her arms with a strength that I had almost forgotten she possessed; it is the strength born of hard work and worry, and holding a child safe even when they struggle.

'I do not doubt it,' she says, again, and I wish she had not. She sounds so much less certain with repetition.

* * *

Three men stand before me and ask their questions.

I sit in the front pew of the church, my hands folded demurely in my lap, my eyes downcast. I know better than to show my true face, or give my answers.

My father, Mr Redmore, Reverend Mountcastle: they have all read the letters that Mr Tiller sent to me. I handed them over as soon as we were gathered in the church. Reverend Mountcastle holds them now; the once-white pages, folded, look grubby, the edges curling. 'Why did you not inform your father of these improper advances? You must have known it was your duty.'

'I am sorry,' I whisper, which goes nowhere towards answering his question but at least seems to mollify him. He stands in the centre of the aisle; behind him are the carved wooden steps to his pulpit and the long stained-glass window of Mary in blue, with the baby Jesus in her arms.

My father is on Reverend Mountcastle's left. His arms are crossed and his mouth straight. His cheeks appear to be permanently flushed since my revelation, as if they will never overcome the embarrassment of it.

On the right of the Reverend stands Mr Redmore. This must be his first time in church since that Sunday he attended upon his return from the war. His eyes do not look so kindly upon me any more. I feel my body trembling, and I cannot control it.

'It is very troubling that you kept it secret, Shirley,' says the Reverend. 'You were always a sensible girl. Where has that sensible girl gone?'

'I was – charmed,' I say.

I have spent hours preparing this as my line of defence. Let them think I was weak-minded, and Mr Tiller took advantage of me with stories that a real man would not possibly entertain.

'But now you see clearly?'

'Yes, sir.'

'I don't understand it, I just don't understand it,' he mutters. 'It is very strange indeed, this talk of rocks and future plans, and the letters are – well, they are deeply disturbing, do you not think so?' He appeals to my father, who obliges, through clenched teeth.

'I do.' The sight of him standing there, saying those particular words in such clipped severity when this should be my own wedding rehearsal, touches a deep nerve of quixotic humour within me that cannot be repressed.

'She smiles,' says Mr Redmore. 'She's smiling. She finds this laughable, while my son fancies himself broken-hearted.'

'Perhaps it is a sign of the befuddlement,' says my father,

who has leapt at the possible explanation as I knew he would. 'She has long been thick with the man, and I knew it was not normal in nature, but her mother told me she could settle it with delicacy.'

'Well, it seems not.' Mountcastle sighs.

'It's all some fantasy caused by the war,' adds the blacksmith. 'Men come back with the strangest tales, and think they face enemies, seeing them in every place. Once you have lived through such times you cannot dismiss them. The man is ill.'

'Does that mean we should forgive him?' says my father, outraged.

'We should forgive everyone as best we can in the name of Christian duty,' states the Reverend. 'But forgiveness does not mean forgetfulness. Tiller must not be put in charge of young minds, or even allowed near to them, that much is obvious.'

They do not ask me why I chose to believe Mr Tiller, or what I have seen with my own eyes. They do not include me in this conversation at all.

It does not matter; it does not matter! I have outwitted Mr Tiller. He will be forced out of the village in shame and penury, and if he applies for work in this county news of it will reach Westerbridge. He will not be able to harm Daniel, and his ability to affect the future of others will be seriously diminished.

'Do we agree that the man is touched?' asks Mountcastle.

'I do not care much one way or the other, but he must pay for what he has done.' My father's arms remain crossed. I am glad I asked my mother to leave us at the church door; she would set about the business of placating him, as if it were her duty, and I need him to be angry enough to ensure the downfall of Mr Tiller.

'But what exactly has he done?' says the Reverend. I keep my eyes cast down, and pretend I am too ashamed to even look at them.

There is a silence, and then I hear footsteps. The Reverend sits beside me in the pew, and places a hand on mine. I have never been so close to him. He smells strange, musty. Underneath his vestments he is just another old man. I hold my breath.

'Shirley,' he says, gently. 'You were alone with Mr Tiller on numerous occasions, were you not? You helped him with tasks, such as the organisation of the May Day celebrations, is that not right?'

'That is right, sir.'

'Yes, that's right. You see, I already know this because he told me what a great help you were to him, and suggested you should be May Queen because of it. He has always thought highly of you, hasn't he?'

'Yes, sir.'

'Good. Good.' Mountcastle pats my head. Why does he feel so free to do so? I have not encouraged him. 'Did Mr Tiller ever kiss you?' he says, loudly, so the other men can hear, I assume. 'With his mouth?'

One wonders how else a person could kiss another. 'No, sir,' I say.

'Did he ever put his hands upon you?'

'No, sir.'

'Very well. Thank you.'

Here is my moment. My mother called me brave, and I must prove her right. 'I put my hands upon him.'

The Reverend's hand becomes a dead weight on mine. I would throw it off if I could.

'Indeed?' he says, finally. Mr Redmore and my father do not move. 'How so?'

'He took off his shirt, and I touched his skin. We were alone, in his cottage. I cannot say more. Do not make me say more.' I close my eyes and hunch my shoulders, as if emotion has overwhelmed me. I have learned that words are worth less than tears.

'And so now we understand why you have called off your wedding. Oh Shirley.'

My father is murmuring under his breath and I raise my head to see him deep in his fury, Mr Redmore already moving to his side.

'Calm yourself,' says the blacksmith. 'Calm yourself.'

'I will kill him,' states my father, icy with anger.

'This is a church, Frederick Fearn,' barks the Reverend. Oh, the three of them are fast becoming their own stage act; they only need me to be the cause and the audience.

'He should answer for this!' shouts my father, and his eyes pass over me as if I am not there at all.

'And he will. We will track him down, and he will see justice.'

'He will be miles away already,' says Mr Redmore. 'If the girl had not seen fit to delay telling us, we could have—'

'If you had not told all that the engagement was broken, he would not have had the chance to run!'

I hold up my hand. None of this makes sense to me, and now my stomach has a strange sensation within it, as if wheels are turning fast within. 'Could you explain, sir?' I ask the Reverend. 'I don't understand.'

All three of them grimace. I am an annoyance to have interrupted. 'He has left the village,' says my father. 'Your precious schoolmaster made off this morning.'

'How... how do you know this?'

'We have been asking door to door about one of the girls in the village who has seen fit to run away,' says Reverend Mountcastle. 'I called in on Mr Tiller myself this morning, and found the cottage empty. Now I understand why. He would have heard in the village last night that you had broken your engagement, as Mr Redmore saw fit to tell all while in his cups at The Three Crowns.'

'My boy is broken-hearted,' repeats Mr Redmore.

'You all knew,' I breathe. 'You knew, and you waited for me to speak of it first. And now...'

Reverend Mountcastle looks at me with pity. 'This is Westerbridge, girl. Did you forget how news spreads here? Even the news you would rather not have known?'

I do not believe Mr Tiller has simply run away. He is fervent, unswayable. What has he done with the extra time given to him through other people's gossip? What have I made him desperate enough to do?

The Reverend leaves me, and walks back to make the group of three once more. They talk amongst themselves, and I am excluded from their conversation. I am so very unimportant. There is no power left in me.

I gaze up at the stained-glass window. The blue of Mary's robe is soft and light. She holds the infant Jesus so gently, and around her head is a halo, the white light blending with her beautiful golden hair. Jesus is the centre of the picture, of course. His sweet expression dominates all. The blue of the robe simply frames him, in his promise of perfection. The mother does not matter, and yet he could not exist without her. As no man can exist without a woman to bear him.

I stand up.

'The girl who has run away,' I say. 'Who was it?'

My father waves me into silence.

'No!' I shout, and they all turn to me. I will make them hear, just this once. I will have a clear answer. 'Who was it?'

'Phyllis Clemens, the baker's girl. Now sit down, and— Shirley!'

But I am off, and running. Mr Tiller has left the village because his job is done, and he has won this war.

* * *

I must hope that he has taken her with him. And yet my heart tells me that he would not burden himself with her, not when he has a future to save. What would one more girl matter to him? But she is so pretty; how could he look at her golden hair and see only a problem to be solved? Surely he would be moved at the sight of her, and take her along as he fled.

I am now more rock than flesh, he wrote to me.

Out of the churchyard, past the houses of the poor, down the lane where the branches grow thick overhead, and here I am at Mr Tiller's cottage. Perhaps Phyllis is inside, locked up in a back room, or perhaps there is a letter. Yes, a letter, one last missive from Mr Tiller in which he reprimands me for not keeping my promises, and gives me one final chance to keep to my end of the bargain. *I have abducted Phyllis Clemen*s, the letter will say. *I will return her once you are married.*

At first the cottage door does not admit me, but when I put my shoulder to it, the wood squeals and it swings back. There can be no doubt that he has gone. Already the hall feels damp and unwelcoming. In the kitchen, the furniture remains while all personal touches are gone. The tea chest no longer stands beside the dresser; how could he have taken it? He must have hired a horse and cart from somewhere. No doubt the village will be full of the details.

The lamp, unlit, still sits by the window. There is no letter on the table. I had envisioned it so very clearly. But it is not there.

I search all the rooms for some sign, some portent, of his plans. The living room is as bare and cold as a prison. The mattress upon his bed is stripped and discoloured, and the room bears the smell of mildew. I open the window and look down upon his wild garden, the roses now done with, the vegetable plots thick with tangling weeds. Beyond that, I catch a glimpse of the bridge and the river.

I walk down the narrow stairs, and leave the cottage behind me. I make my way to the bridge. If Mr Tiller wanted to leave me a message, is that where he would put it? That is where we stood and saw each other clearly for the first time.

Upon the bridge, leaning against the stone wall, I look down at the water. I feel his desire to let me know he is disgusted with me. It is early afternoon and the frogs are not singing. The crickets do not call. A peculiar silence has stretched over the animals and insects.

There she is.

There is her golden hair, flowing with the water, spooling out from under the bridge. I climb down to the hidden shelter where the children thought the adults would not go, and I see her in the mud, her hair carried over her face, her skin blue-white and her neck a mess of purple marks where he squeezed her dry.

He has left his message.

* * *

My mother's plan involves taking only that which I can carry, and the letter she has written to her parents in which she asks them to feed me and clothe me for a while. In exchange, she writes, I am a good worker. Although she does not say at what.

My plan deviates somewhat, but it starts out in the same

manner; it is dawn, and I am walking down the lower field towards the stile, and the road, moving apace so that I will make good distance before my father notes my absence.

I will go to Taunton, and then beyond. I will look for word of either Mr Tiller (although the police are hard at work to find him too, of course) or of a rock that gives visions of a future that many would say does not concern me. But I say that it does.

I reach the stile, and find Daniel Redmore waiting for me. I stare at him, and he stares back.

'How did you—'

'Your mother,' he says.

'It was not her business to tell you.'

'It's all somebody else's business until you make it your own,' he says, and it is very hard to argue with that.

He is looking handsome in the early morning light, his hair unkempt, shivering in his shirt sleeves, and it is intriguing to see him astride a bicycle. I did not know he could ride one. This one has two seats; the one behind him is free.

'It's a tandem,' he says, helpfully.

'I can see that.'

'It cost all my money. I bought it for us, when—back when—' He takes a gasp of air, and then says, in a rush, 'I am so sorry that I told my father, but I could not make sense of it, and some things are difficult to hide,'

'I know. I know that now. I should not have asked it of you. Nobody should keep secrets for another, I suspect. It does the world no good at all.'

'I'm to take you to your grandparents until after the funeral and the police catch…' His words peter out. Heaven knows how the murder has affected him, although whether he chooses to make it the centre of his life is entirely up to him, of course. How hard-hearted I have become in my thinking. I even surprise myself with how much I have changed from that foolish girl who fancied herself in love.

'I'm not going that way. I'm going to Taunton.'

He squints up at the sky. 'This sounds like an old daydream come back to life.'

'It is far from that.'

'Well, let me get you there. And further, if you want.'

I shake my head. 'You have no inkling of what you're getting yourself into.'

'You could explain it to me as we ride. It's a long way to Taunton.'

'I could try, I suppose, as long as you pay attention.'

'Well,' he says, as I struggle with my skirts so that I can climb on to the second saddle, 'just as long as you don't write it down. It seems to me all the troubles come when people start writing things down.'

He is filled with good sense today, and we push off together with the right foot, and only wobble a little on the first mile. Cycling comes naturally to me.

I split my attention between the morning sun over the hills and the contours of Daniel's beautiful back. His presence gives me an optimism I have not felt in months.

I will find the other rocks, and I will smash them all. I will wage war against those that deem me, and others like me, unimportant.

I will fight to make this world a better one.

ACKNOWLEDGEMENTS

First up, thanks to my personal rocks: Nick, Elsa and Harley.

I'm glad to get an opportunity to thank everyone who worked on this book and did such a brilliant job. That goes for Jana Heidersdorf, Rob Clark, Martin Cox, Gary Budden, Henry Dillon and George Sandison.

This being a book about teachers, I'd also like to say thank you to some great teachers I know and admire. They include Peter and Eileen Whiteley, Helen Whiteley, Rebecca Denton, and David Ian Rabey.

For those people who teach me and have taught me how to be a good friend, writer, or person through example – thank you: Jim Ovey, Neil Ayres, Tim Stretton and all the MNWers, George Sandison again, John Griffiths, Anna Wanigasekara, Rob Kemp, and the one-woman Crafty Revolution and hostess extraordinaire who was Francesca Kemp. I miss you Fran.

READ ON FOR A

BRAND-NEW
SHORT STORY

by
ALIYA
WHITELEY

THE
LAST VOYAGE
OF THE
SMILING
HENRY

The captain of the Fair Arthur, upon return to the port of New Bristol, reported forthwith to Worthington Hall, mindful of the money she had been promised for the news she could bring.

There she described a sighting of vast spewing volcanoes, visible to the naked eye as erupting gouts of red upon the horizon, and took her payment in exchange for their position marked upon a chart of the Northern Ocean before departing for the nearest tavern.

Later that evening, Isabella switched her attention back and forth from the chart to her mother's notes within the peace of the family home's library. The cracked spines of many leather tomes surrounded her, and each recorded some adventure from the line of Worthington. Here was the very desk where her mother had sat and speculated upon the cooling of lava to form crenulated rocks; it was as the latest Lady Worthington had claimed ten years ago. The map and co-ordinates matched those drawn in the captain's own shaky, sea-aged hand.

Could such torrents make an island, newly born to the world? Ten years had passed since her mother had set off upon a voyage to prove her theory, and Isabella remembered little of the stages of preparation for the journey, being only seven years of age at the time. She did, however, have a clear memory of being shown the flag, unfurled, that her mother intended to plant. Scarlet with a silver dragon upon it, it had mesmerised her as her mother raised it high, brandishing with pride the stout pole to which it was attached.

'We will own an island,' her mother had said. 'It will bear the Worthington coat of arms, my dear.' And then there was the trip to the docks in the carriage, and waving goodbye. Then cakes with her father afterwards in an establishment that smelled of coffee and the sea, bitter and tangy and strange to her nursery-reared nostrils.

Isabella did not remember being informed that her mother's ship – The Adventuress – had been lost at sea, with no trace of it found. She only remembered her father crying, the tresses of his hair in disarray, and her childish reassurances to him that, one day, all would be mended.

She was no longer a child. The day had come; she had her confirmation, and the time for her to make good on her promise to her father was nigh.

* * *

'He could have at least made the effort just this once,' said her personal womanservant and confidante, Samantha, while brushing down Isabella's jacket for dinner.

'You know how father suffers with his nerves. We had a quiet farewell last night, and he was in good spirits, and hopeful. I'm content with that.' Isabella had decided not to tell Samantha about the tears Father had cried, or his pleas for her not to follow in her mother's footsteps. It was beyond her to speak of his desperation without crying herself, and she could not bear for anyone to see the tracks of tears upon her cheeks and think her weak. Not at this crucial moment when gaining the respect of the crew was vital.

'You're ready,' said Samantha, adjusting the lapels of the jacket and then eyeing Isabella up and down. 'Enjoy dinner with your fine captain and first officer, both of whom look capable of providing good conversation on the topics of scurvy and rigging, and not much else. I will stay here and mend your socks yet again. Lucky me. I would swear you forget to trim your toenails in order to create little holes in the toes for the sole purpose of vexing me.'

'I would have thought an early night would have suited you, since you always claim to be on the point of exhaustion,' Isabella pointed out, but not without good humour. Sparring with Samantha was a comfortable reassurance in this unfamiliar place.

She spared a last look around the cabin that would be her home in the coming months. It was utilitarian, yet had everything she needed for the journey, and the small bed – so different from her canopied four-poster at Worthington Hall – would make for an interesting change. Unfrilled and uncomplicated, this sailor's life, she thought, and the pleasant rocking of the Smiling Henry upon the sea did not trouble her, although she suspected it was already vexing

Samantha for in truth she was even grumpier than usual.

The captain's steward (a girl who could not have been more than ten years old and went by the inexplicable name of Barndoor) waited outside the creaking wooden door to escort Isabella to the Great Cabin, where the captain and the first officer shook her hand solemnly, and bade her sit and eat from the vast, polished table laden with roast goose and all the trimmings one associated with a fine lady's meal.

They were excellent company, choosing to talk not of business but of their journeys together upon the Smiling Henry to places both wondrous and strange, and Isabella was relieved to see how clearly they valued each other's company and expertise, for she had read that those who travel at sea together should be as sisters in arms, facing the perils of the deep blue with interlocked arms.

Captain Bird was a sturdy figure of a woman, with blue-grey eyes and a crest of white hair, so that she resembled the ocean itself from its steely depths below to its exuberant waves above. 'And now,' she said, as Barndoor cleared away the remains of dinner, 'tell us of this place we sail to, and give us some warning of what we might expect to find there.'

'In truth, Captain, I do not know. My mother's journal spoke only of her own suppositions; new land, formed of lava, too young for life to grow upon it. No vegetation, no drinking water, perhaps still molten hot, and steaming where black rocks clash with the icy sea of the north. This could be a perilous undertaking.'

'That is why you have paid us well, and we have made

provisions for many outcomes, Miss Worthington. But surely you are aware that the picture you paint of a nightmarish land means that there can be no hope for the survival of your mother? And no chance of finding her body, either, I'd venture.'

'Chances are the fish or birds will have done away with any trace in the decade that has passed,' observed First Officer Valentino, who was a grizzled sailor herself, and obviously used to plainer speech. But it was a relief to know they wished to discuss the matter without varnish or vanity.

'Indeed,' said Isabella. 'No, I do not expect to find her alive or otherwise. I only wish to finish what she started, for the sake of her soul, which I am certain cannot be at rest until a Worthington flag has claimed land and written itself forevermore on the maps of this planet, whose secrets are yet to be fully unlocked.'

'The spirit of adventure passes from generation to generation,' said Captain Bird, gravely, 'and long may that be so. The lives of our greatest pioneers, the women who ventured far and risked all, sailing space and sea: we salute them all, and continue their work, eschewing easy victories to embrace the precepts of our foremothers.' She raised her glass of wine, and the three made a toast while the proud wooden figurehead of the Smiling Henry plunged on through the waves before him, his carved buxom cheeks and defined pectorals a cheer to all those who sailed in him.

* * *

Samantha's sea-sickness lasted long weeks into the voyage. She complained mightily and refused to leave the cabin except for the occasional midnight stroll around the deck, claiming sleep was impossible before falling into a doze mid-afternoon that could last until dinner time. Anybody would have thought that she is the mistress and I am the servant, thought Isabella, but she refrained from saying it.

The day that the great orange plumes appeared upon the horizon, just as described by the captain of the Fair Arthur, was also the day that Samantha bothered to count her calendar and spoke, in a hushed tone of great excitement, about the possibility of being with child.

'For Heaven's sake!' exclaimed Isabella. 'How ridiculously careless you are!' The two of them stood side by side on the quarter deck, looking out as the gouts of flame climbed into the sky and then fell, climbed and fell, as regular as the waves against the planking of the ship.

Samantha hung her head, but Isabella could tell she was far from despondent about her discovery.

'Well,' said Isabella, 'perhaps all journeys – of the land, the sea, and the internal workings of the body – are laudable, even from the humblest and most unexpected of beginnings.'

'You are quite the wisest of women!' said Samantha, perking up considerably. 'And imagine, a tiny life to be carried within me, on to a new island – is that not fitting?'

There were many replies Isabella could have made, and also many questions that really should have been asked, such as who the father might be, and how a servant might find the income to pay a man to take care of her offspring so that child-rearing would not interfere with her duties. But hey-ho; Samantha's predilection for a cheap trick down by the harbour on her evenings off with one of the local lads for sale was, in all probability, to blame for her condition, and it seemed a trifle ridiculous to plan for a future back in New Bristol when their return was far from guaranteed.

'Yes,' Isabella agreed. 'Most fitting. Now, do you think you could find me some lunch, or is that too arduous a task for you?'

Samantha beamed and set off for the galley. If she had heard the note of castigation in her mistress's voice she had chosen to ignore it, and that was one of the reasons why Isabella loved her so. Besides, she did look very well indeed with the bloom of impending motherhood upon her. And if she decided later that such a tie did not appeal, well, a visit to the ship's doctor (who would be used to such inconveniences on board) would take care of it.

* * *

Onwards, onwards, into the night, up and down on the swell of the sea, with the vast columns of falling flame drawing ever closer: Isabella stood on the prow as the crew worked, singing in their lusty voices of the men they had loved and lost, even if only for one cold night upon dry land. The longing for warm male arms was upon them all, particularly as those huge plumes of lava illuminated the night sky, and tested the resolve of even the most experienced sailor.

'I don't like it,' First Officer Valentino had stated over dinner. 'Observation through the eyeglass shows that the sea moves strangely around these eruptions; I cannot read the tides, nor see a clear path for our sailing. There are rocks, for certain, and yet their position seems to change so that the crests of the waves break and fall in forms that are unreadable to me.'

The captain had absorbed these words with a slow nod. 'And yet we must draw closer,' she said. 'Do you think it possible?'

Isabella held her breath during the exchange. It was only when Valentino had said, 'Closer, yes, close enough to see if land has formed beneath,' that she dared to let out a sigh, and hope.

'Put Piker on helmslady duties,' Captain Bird had said. 'She'll steer Henry right. Heartbow on lookout – that girl has the sharpest eyes that ever sailed this ocean.'

And so Isabella watched Piker and Heartbow and the others hard at work, bringing her ever closer to the path her mother took, and to her own destiny. She yearned for it. She leaned towards it, breathing deep of the cold, salty air, until her eyes would not stay open of their own accord.

Then she returned to her cabin to find Samantha already snoring. Surely sleep could not find her, between the loud, grating breaths of her womanservant and the excitement that made her heart pound with equal clamour. No, no, she would never sleep, it surely would not come to her, she would like awake until the first light of –

* * *

Morning, thought Isabella, stirring in her small bed to find the day had arrived.

Or had it? The quality of light through the porthole, next to Samantha's sleeping form, had an unnatural yellow tinge to it that turned her plump face sickly. *A mask of disease*, Isabella thought, and then had to reach over to shake her womanservant awake.

'Hmph,' said Samantha, then, 'What?'

'The light. The light is wrong.'

'Too early.'

'No, it's late,' said Isabella, and felt the truth of her words. The hour was indeed late; they had overslept, and the rousing sounds of the ship's business had not reached them. Instead all was silent where voices and song should have aided the passage of the day.

The view from the porthole afforded no answer. There was a greasy quality to the air, but the view, on the opposite side from the lava spews, was of a calm, unchanged sea.

'Something is awry,' said Isabella.

They dressed quickly. Leaving the cabin took a great deal of courage, and yet more was needed to make their way up to the quarter deck. Holding hands, they stepped forth, and the world into which they emerged was truly not the one they had left.

A few women worked on, but their business was far from sailing. They carried and laid out the bodies of their compatriots in long rows upon the poop deck. How could so many have fallen without a single sound reaching Isabella's ears? And so many had not yet been arranged to order. They lay quite still, scattered, their limbs in odd positions, their hands formed into rigid claws. Isabella tore her gaze away, up to the sky, and found her gaze meeting poor inverted Heartbow, fallen to tangle in the rigging of the Mainsail, swaying in time with the swell of the sea. Her dangling arms revealed the same clawed fingers, and her eyes and mouth were open, black and staring, staring at a horror unknown.

'Look away,' said Samantha. 'Look away.' And she attempted to drag Isabella back from the bodies of those who had sailed *Henry* with such skill.

'They are all dead,' Isabella said, with wonder, 'How can that be? How –?'

The portly figure of First Officer Valentino disengaged from the act of organising the dead and came to their side, her hair dishevelled, her jacket unbuttoned. Still, she straightened and gave a small bow before clasping their hands warmly. 'You are alive! Two more of us. Thank the Heavens. By my calculations that makes twelve of us.'

'Twelve? From a crew of...'

'Eighty,' said Valentino, and her agony at the loss pulled at her sturdy features for a moment before she pressed on. 'It was a noxious cloud that passed across the ship just after daybreak. Piker was attempting to steer a true course through these evil waters.' She broke off to spit upon the deck. 'Forgive me. A sudden change in the wind brought a thick, sulphurous mist upon us that drifted square across the ship, penetrating all the decks to bring a swift, choking death to all who breathed it. It was sheer chance that spared some; I, myself, saw the cloud pass mere inches from my nose as I stood beside Piker at the Helm. She coughed, choked, slumped forward. I could not move; all was so sudden, the terror of it...' Valentino's voice grew hoarse, but she pushed on, determined to tell her story. 'I did not attempt to aid her, and that is my greatest guilt and also my salvation, for the cloud passed, and I lived, and she died. So many died, so many! I cannot understand.'

'Captain Bird?' asked Samantha.

Valentino shook her head.

Dreadful, dreadful; the nature of their predicament began to dawn upon Isabella. The steady hand of the Captain was lost, and so few sailors remained.

'Can the *Henry* still be sailed?' she asked.

'Perhaps. If we all pull our weight.' Valentino eyed Samantha thoughtfully. 'But without experienced sailors, I doubt our chances of seeing New Bristol again.'

Isabella gazed out upon the sea, and saw the fateful orange plumes shooting skywards; for a moment she fancied she could feel their heat upon her face.

'They have moved again,' said Valentino, 'and look there.' She pointed, and Isabella's eyes sought out a strange sight indeed. For there was land – or, at least, an outcropping of black rock that rose to a central peak. They were close enough to see the jagged outline of the mountain that dominated the new island. 'It sprung into existence overnight. The terrible mist claimed its victims, and then cleared to reveal it.'

'How can that be so?'

'I have no answer for you, Miss Worthington. I have no answer for any of these happenings.'

Seeing land – any land – was a welcome sight at that moment, but the crags and pinnacles of the jutting mountain were undeniably bleak to look upon. It seemed a most unwelcoming addition of land to the world.

'Look at the peak,' said Valentino. At the highest point of the mountain there were circling white specks, barely visible.

'Birds,' said Samantha. 'Birds fly there. What does it mean?'

'Seabirds fly upon warm currents of air; beyond that, I do not know.'

'Perhaps they can see something we cannot from this flat vantage point. This island holds more than one mystery, I think.' The desire to stand upon the land was strong in her, as was her spirit of adventure, unquenched even in the presence of death.

'You think we should –'

'We are here. We cannot sail on at this moment, until the dead are disposed of and instructions are given. Perhaps there is something on this island to give us a solution, or some hope.'

Valentino and Samantha exchanged wary looks. 'What possible hope can there be?'

A saying of her mother's came to Isabella, then. She repeated the words out loud, taking comfort from them: 'Hope, relief, and adventure: the three often appear together, and in the strangest of places. All that is needed is to seek them out.'

Perhaps it was the thought of having to squarely face the despondency of their situation that swayed Valentino and Samantha to acquiesce. Valentino mustered together a small landing party while leaving a few behind to catalogue the dead before their bodies could be submitted to the sea. Then she gave orders for a Launch to be prepared and loaded with provisions for immediate departure.

* * *

Barndoor had survived the toxic cloud, being tucked away asleep in the corner of the Grand Cabin; Isabella took great comfort in that handsome face, opposite her own position within the Launch. The familiarity of those blue eyes soothed Isabella's nerves, even as Samantha – seated beside her – clenched her hand hard in worry.

The sailors chosen to woman the oars did their job well. Isabella had taken care to memorise their names as Valentino instructed them; Harkin, Pinch, Ramsgate and Attwater looked a capable foursome even though they had suffered a terrible loss, for a crew was undoubtedly a family, and a ship a home.

Valentino herself, at the stern of the Launch, was deep in thought, and behind her was the view of the *Smiling Henry*. It receded as the sailors rowed their hardest, until it looked so small; and from this distance, Isabella thought, nothing looked awry. How far it had sailed over the years, only to have tragedy befall it. Would it sail again?

Isabella turned upon the wooden bench that was her seat and saw the craggy shore drawing close. The waves became choppy, and broke around the Launch, and the force of the motion overtook the rowers' actions. The oars were put away, and Valentino leaped from the stern to stand chest deep in the water. The sailors followed suit, and the business began of guiding the boat on to the shore ahead, which appeared to be a beach of grey sand nestled between two outcroppings of jagged rocks.

After a moment's hesitation Isabella followed suit, dropping into the sea to find it as warm as a bath; she grabbed the side of the Launch and pulled as best she could while Samantha and Barndoor stared at her. The force of the waves was powerful, nearly knocking her from her feet with each surge forwards, but she stood firm, and did not let go of the Launch until it was far up the beach and safe from the whims of the tide.

How fine the grey sand was, as powdery as ash, flying up around their bodies as they collapsed upon it. Odd curves and arcs made a complex pattern, permeated by small holes in its surface. Isabella lay stretched out, fighting to control her breath, and saw the peak overhead, and the birds that circled it. How tall and imposing it looked; would the summit be attainable in the hours left before sundown? They would have to set a fast pace over the rocks and scree that led up at a steep incline, and the sun was at its highest in the sky.

Still, she had no doubt that her Worthington determination would see her through. She stood, fighting off fatigue, and approached Valentino, who was deep in thought herself, facing the sea, her eyes fixed upon the *Smiling Henry*.

'Shall we commence?'

Valentino turned, her eyes troubled, to survey the mountain. 'I do not understand any of this.'

'I have a gut feeling, and that is all,' Isabella said. 'You have sailed far on such feelings. Am I correct?'

'You are. And since I have no captain, and no notion of what can be done, I will trust your feeling, Miss Worthington. I will organise the women and provisions.'

'Very well. Five minutes, then.'

Isabella walked away, and found Samantha still sitting in the Launch, looking despondent, with the wide-eyed Barndoor keeping her company. 'I need you both to take care of a most important task,' she told them.

'Which is?' said Samantha.

'Stay here. Guard the boat. We will return forthwith.'

Barndoor promised to do that very thing, while Samantha slumped in relief.

The climb commenced, and every so often Isabella would

look back to the beach and see the two of them pattering about upon the sand, looking for all the world like a mother and daughter on holiday, about to launch into a game of rough and tumble.

* * *

How bizarre the world is, she thought as she pushed onwards, leading the way, with sweat streaming between her shoulder blades and soaking through her shirt, *bizarre enough to make all action seem quite futile, if I am not careful.*

And yet she strode on, her body working mechanically while her mind struggled to make sense of her actions. The cries of the birds became audible, then grew louder, and their identity became clear. They were nothing but common seagulls, and they took turns diving down over the mountain, then soaring up to circle once more.

For a time Isabella could not make sense of their actions, until it came to her that they were diving into the heart of the mountain itself – but how could that be? A gull flashed by her; she caught a fine view of its yellow eyes, and the scarlet tinge upon its beak.

All such birds have crimson slashes on their beaks naturally, she reminded herself. *It is not blood. It could not be blood.*

'Look!' called one of the women.

Isabella stopped her relentless climb and straightened up.

They were nearly at the top – and a new swatch of scarlet was plainly visible over the crest of the peak. Scarlet tatters, streaming upwards in the warm wind, with a silver dragon visible upon it: the Worthington flag, standing proud, although ripped and stained with guano.

Isabella felt the knowledge rip through her as ecstatic pain – her mother had stood at that very spot, and planted the flag firm. There could be no other explanation. Her energy renewed, she scrambled the last few feet and was rewarded with a view of such incongruity that she could not begin to reconcile it.

Life!

Green, verdant life within the mountain, for the peak was only the highest point along the craggy mouth of a crater, and leafy vegetation lined the sides and plunged down into its heart. This was not a mountain but a volcano, except fiery oblivion did not inhabit it. Instead, plants grew, springing up thick and heavy, and the seagulls were swooping low to get to the clean fresh water that must encourage the fecundity. It was a miraculous view over a great forest, with its very growth obscuring a further view to its floor, and Isabella heard the gasps of surprise of the others as they joined her, and then fanned out to explore the rim of the crater.

And the flag, the flag too amazed her. She crossed to it and placed a hand upon its stout pole. 'Worthington Island,' she said, relishing the words. For surely her mother would have spoken those words too, a decade earlier.

'Steps!' called Valentino. 'Steps downwards, carved from the rock itself.'

Yes, impossibly, there were rough-hewn steps, creating a circular staircase down into the crater-forest, and onwards to discovery. Her mother's remains, perhaps, or even – could she be – alive? Kept well? Could there be indigenous people making ingress to this volcano? In such a place it was possible to believe anything.

She took the lead once more, and they set off in single file, pressing their bodies against the rock as they descended. Liquid streamed down the rock face in rivulets; where sweat had once soaked her clothes, now Isabella found herself soaked through in clear, sweet water, for when she sucked at the sleeve of her shirt she found it drinkable, and deliciously so.

The leaves and foliage pressed close around her, and had to be pushed aside at times. How angular these blades of greenery were, and slick to the touch, like cool metal daggers. They were, Isabella realised, not familiar to her. She was no expert upon horticultural matters, but such sharp, pointed flora that could cut at the skin certainly did not resemble the plump flowers and growths from the garden at Worthington Hall. The further they walked, the spikier and more unwelcoming the leaves seemed to be, until she was relieved to find a ledge where she could pause and examine the thin bloody lines across her palms.

'Looks painful,' said Valentino, coming to her side.

'In truth, they do not hurt, but they bleed freely.' She

looked downwards. The stairs carried on into a darkness from which strange noises emanated: clicks and squeals that spoke of the existence of insects and perhaps other forms of animal life.

'We will not make it back to the Henry for nightfall if we do not turn back now.'

'I know, and yet... you saw the flag,' said Isabella. 'How can we turn back, knowing –'

A sharp cry interrupted her words; she looked up and saw one of the sailors, pressing herself against the rock face, clutching her upper arm as blood streamed from between her fingers.

'Attwater,' called Valentino, 'What happened, woman?'

'The branch – it swayed towards me, right towards me, and cut me deep,' cried Attwater. Her colleagues rushed to her as she swayed, and steadied her. One of them ripped the sleeve from her own shirt and began to wrap the material around the wound.

'Steady now. Are you sure it – moved? There's no wind down here.'

'It came for me, I swear it,' Attwater said in a rush of terror. 'It wanted blood.'

Was it her imagination, or did the foliage seem to be crowding closer upon these words? Isabella shook her head; no, no, it was not the fault of the words, but of the blood dripping from their wounds. She watched in horror as the nearest plant to her damaged hands strained forward, inching towards the thin slices through her flesh.

'Retreat!' she shouted. 'Retreat!' But Attwater could not hurry, and the plants seemed somehow to feel the sailor's weakness; the forest came to life, uncurling tendrils and vines that reached out and wrapped themselves around the screaming woman, plucking her from where she crouched to lift her from the staircase.

'Aid her! Aid her!' cried Valentino, but they had no weapons between them, and in moments she was lost to them, dragged down into the darkness beneath, from which a cacophony of shrieks and tickings erupted, and Attwater's own screams were lost within them.

The other sailors moaned, and the plants shivered at their fear and despair; Isabella watched the branches lean forward, felt how human flesh had become the object of their attentions. To escape back up the stairs was impossible; they would soon tire and be picked off – what alternative could she find?

To go down, down, downwards, and there... a hole, not far beneath them, possibly a cave? Could it act as a place of refuge? 'Follow me!' she cried out, and took the steps at great speed, ignoring the stings and slaps of the cutting leaves that reached for her, before plunging into the opening in the rock face to be met with a cold blackness that, for a heartbeat, seemed to her to be death itself.

But, no, she was not dead. And nor was Valentino, who followed her in and collided with her; they clung to each other, shivering, as Valentino called for the others, and received response.

'Harkin!'

'Here,' said a shaken voice, 'Here.'

'Pinch!'

To that, there was no response. Valentino tried once more, and then, with dread thick in her throat, 'Ramsgate?'

No reply to that name, either. Valentino sobbed once, then fell silent.

'Have we a tinderbox?' asked Isabella.

'I have,' said Harkin. 'In my pack.' There were rustling movements, then a most welcome warm yellow light flooded the cave. Isabella cast her eyes first over Harkin, sweating and breathing hard in her fear, holding the small candle in her hand.

'Good lass,' said Isabella. 'Now, where we are?' It was a large space, easily big enough for many women to stand upright, and as they moved further within its treasures were revealed. For the candle illuminated thick veins of glittering metal within the rock, beautiful and twisted and rich in colour.

'Gold!' said Harkin. 'I'll wager that's gold.'

They pressed on with their explorations, and soon began to find strange carvings made of an unknown substance, spongy and dull. The figures depicted were short and squat, naked, and all male. Their appendages were elongated and stood erect, and their bearing was proud. Some of the figures even carried sticks that had been pushed into the material, brandishing them as weapons. 'A race of man-warriors?' murmured Valentino. 'This is strange indeed.'

But Isabella's attention was fixed upon their final gruesome discovery: a human form, lying upon her side, eyes closed as if in sleep. Isabella gazed upon the peaceful features of her mother, Lady Endeavour Worthington.

Dead, yes, already departed from this world: the skin was desiccated, leathery, but intact. Mummified. Neither moisture nor the plants had penetrated the cave. She fell to her knees by her mother's side and touched her hair, grey where once a rich shock of brown curls had grown.

'Mother,' she whispered. 'I have found you. I have found you.'

And more, for upon her chest was a small notebook, and a pencil still in her lifeless grip. Isabella took the small journal and passed it wordlessly to Valentino, and used the rays of candlelight to scan the contents.

'This is indeed Worthington Island, then,' said Harkin. 'She must have been a brave adventurer.'

'The bravest,' replied Isabella. She slipped the wedding ring from her mother's finger and pocketed it. If she somehow found a way to return to her father, he would take comfort in knowing the events surrounding his wife's death. If not, it would remain in her care until her own death, whenever that may be.

'Valentino,' Isabella whispered, but the first officer was reading, lost in the words.

'Let me read on,' said the grizzled seafarer, who appeared to be recovering some of her stalwart character. 'For there are many wonders in this little book that may yet save us.'

'Does the book speak of the plants? I wonder why the plants grow so,' muttered Harkin. 'For where plants that feed on blood grow strong, one must wonder what creature they feed upon, and what eats them in turn.'

'What kind of creature, indeed?'

'Not a creature,' said Valentino. 'Creatures. Look.' She held up the book, and Isabella and Harkin came to cluster around it and stare at the pencil drawing upon the page. Long spikes, Isabella saw at first, not unlike the sharp leaves outside the cave, but closer examination proved these to be segmented worms, sketched carefully, but each one with a stiff, pointed head that formed a spike. Valentino turned the pages to reveal more drawings and notes on these worms, showing them burrowing through foliage, through sand, through anything that stood in their path. Flesh would present no barrier to such a hideous creation.

'Lady Worthington writes of them joining their bodies at night, turning themselves into huge churning cylinders that cut through the undergrowth as it tries to defend itself with its daggerlike leaves,' said Valentino. 'Her party came across the steps within this crater, and found this cave and the remains of a past civilisation within it. Listen to what she writes here…

'"The carnivorous plants quickly got a taste for our flesh, but do not penetrate the cave. Neither do the worms, who seem to shrink from the gold within the rocks. Still, we had to risk venturing outside to hunt for sustenance. All we found was death. Death from the cuts of the leaves, and the hideous churning worms in the darkness. Only this cave and the sea provide a safe place – for neither the worms nor the plants can abide salt water."'

'The worms only move at night,' Isabella said slowly, after further study of the notebook. 'My mother, the last of her party, hid here from them and met her end anyway, through starvation or exhaustion perhaps. Look how serene she is in death. She, at least, met no violent end, eaten alive in the hours of darkness.'

'Which approach quickly,' said Valentino. 'The worms will be waking.'

Isabella found her thoughts turning to the curious holes in the grey sand that they had found when first alighting upon the island. Yes, the worms would wake – and find Samantha and Barndoor sitting pretty, unaware of the danger.

'We must return to the beach,' said Isabella.

'Wait, wait! We cannot go out there,' Valentino cried. 'We will never make it back up the stairs.'

'What, then?' said Harkin.

'Salt water,' said Isabella. 'Both the plants and the worms shy away from it.'

'Yes. That's right. That's right.' Valentino searched in her own pack, and brought forth a skin of water and a small brass container that, to Isabella's surprise, contained fat white crystals of salt. 'I have sailed to the hottest places of this world and found that women can die just for want of a little salt in their diet. I vowed never to be unprepared again.'

'Valentino, you are a wonder!' They mixed the salt and water together, and poured it over their bodies. 'And now, run, run fast, for we must make the top before the heat of the waning sun dries us,' instructed Isabella.

'No, no, I cannot, I cannot...' moaned Harkin, but Valentino cried, 'Do it, woman!' and she obeyed her officer with the instinctive reaction that years of sailing had taught her. The three of them burst from the cave, and began the long climb up the winding stair.

What a journey, upwards and onwards, with the leaves rustling around them, brushing the walls, rubbing against each other to produce a hissing noise of malice; Isabella's breath came hard and fast, her lungs burned with the pain of her charge to freedom, her legs pumped, her eyes soon lost sight of the steps through her tears of exhaustion, but onwards she pushed, even when a single cry reached her ears from behind her, and she knew one of her colleagues had fallen.

But the lip of the crater was reachable, she could make it, she could take the final steps, and there she was, once more with a view out over the sea and of her mother's own planted flag.

She turned to see Valentino emerge, the older woman's breasts heaving against the buttons of her dishevelled uniform. So it had been Harkin's cry that had rung out through the forest. This island – so much older and primaevally brutal than anyone could have suspected – was claiming them, one by one. They had thought it lifeless; on the contrary, it was infused, pervaded by life – horrible, grotesque life that sought to dominate and destroy all other examples of life that it found.

But it will not win, Isabella thought, *I swear it, I swear it.*

She plunged downwards at a reckless speed, making for the beach, and heard Valentino's footsteps behind, following suit.

* * *

The worms had risen from their slumber, and they were too late.

Too late for poor Barndoor, whose body lay under a mass of writhing, feeding abominations as the sun set over the milky sea. Samantha – standing in the sea and sobbing like a boy – watched as they attempted to fight off the creatures, throwing handfuls of sea water upon them, and failed.

When it was clear no more could be done, they hurtled themselves into the sea to stand beside her.

'They emerged from the sand,' she choked out. 'We were playing a game, burying each other, and Barndoor, covered to her waist, said something was biting her, biting her badly, and I scrabbled to pull her free...' She held up her own hands, and Isabella saw the damage that had been wreaked upon them. Missing chunks of flesh, the bites of the worms, were bad enough. But clean through her palm was a hole; the pain must have been excruciating. She put her arm around her womanservant and took her weight.

'We survive,' she told her. 'We wait for morning, and then we take the Launch back to the *Smiling Henry.*'

'Yes,' agreed Samantha, with a wan smile that must have cost her much. 'Yes. I have darned twelve of your socks in an evening; now that is a real horror. I can easily survive this.'

'That's my brave friend,' Isabella said. 'The bravest of us all.'

They watched the worms turn the beach into their playground, a churning mass of nightmares, the cylinders rolling across the sand to form those strange patterns in the sand.

Time wore on.

Stories were told. Valentino repeated the songs that the crew had sung only a day earlier, and Samantha spoke of home, of her father and brothers who would love to take care of the little one inside her while she worked to support them. Thoughts of that masculine calmness, the serenity that the male sex brought to the world, sustained them, somehow, until the worms receded and a beautiful dawn brought pale streaks of pink and orange to the sky.

'Is it safe, do you think, Valentino?' asked Isabella, through a tiredness she had never experienced before. It made the world hazy, unclear to her; she struggled to speak without slurring her words.

'It does not matter,' said Valentino. 'All hope is lost, now.'

'How so? Look, the *Henry* awaits us still.'

'But the Launch does not.'

It was true; the Launch had been penetrated by the worms

and in the soft light of the morning sun the irreparable damage could clearly be seen. So many small holes, chewed through the stout wood – it would not sail again.

'The others, left on board the *Henry* – surely they will come for us?'

'Yes, surely,' echoed Valentino, 'but what is that lick of colour, upon the poop deck? Do you see it?'

'I see it,' said Samantha, her voice calm, as calm as the warm sea in which they still stood. 'It's a fire.'

'How can that be?'

The three of them watched. The fire sprung higher. It grew tall enough to swallow the great mainmast, and the sails, and then the *Henry* began to sink lower, lower, tilting, listing, until it sank slowly from their sight, subsuming to the deep.

They did not speak, for a while.

'I wonder what may have happened to them, while we fought the demons of this island,' said Valentino.

'We will never know.'

Samantha groaned, and doubled over. 'It hurts,' she said. 'The pregnancy. I feel it moving within me.'

'It's too early for such movement.'

'No, the worms, the worms…'

Isabella half-carried her friend to the beach, and laid her down upon the sand, with no choice but to ignore the knowledge of the worms sleeping beneath. 'Did they – penetrate you?'

'I was trying to save Barndoor, and I felt one slide within

me. It has eaten me inside out, eaten my baby, and now it starts on my flesh, I feel it.'

'No, no, that cannot be,' said Isabella, but as she held Samantha in her arms the skin of her stomach tented, then split in a great gush of blood, to reveal the fat segmented body of a well-feasted worm. It slipped out its coils and writhed free, to fall into the sand and burrow to its resting place.

'Do not, do not...' said Isabella, attempting to stem the blood with her hands, to put back the half-eaten organs that bulged from the dreadful wound, but it could not be done, it was hopeless, and Samantha arched her back, sighed, and met her death upon the sand.

* * *

'We are done,' said Valentino. 'There is nothing more this island can do to us.'

They stood upon the sand, the two survivors, and spoke plainly, as only the condemned can. 'Yes, we will die here. Let us hope no others find this accursed place, nor wish to name it. For I was foolish to call it Worthington Island. It is a place for no woman, nor should it bear a woman's name.'

Isabella said prayers over the body of Samantha, and did the same for Barndoor.

'Tell me,' she said, 'why was the girl named so?'

Valentino smiled. 'The story went that her ancestors served with some of the finest captains in history. They travelled the universe, generations on board ships that could sail the stars, and served well. All apart from one ill-fated great-great-aunt, who forgot to secure an airlock while escorting an Admiral on a tour of a newly commissioned warship.'

'That is a terrible mistake for a girl to make,' said Isabella.

'Indeed. The nickname of Barndoor followed her line ever since, along with the common reminder to secure open doors and hatches behind them. Yet each one of the family followed their ancestors into service, and took the teasing and the name with good grace. Why do you think that is so?'

Isabella smiled as the sun rose higher, and the fiery plumes of the volcanoes that had led her to her fate erupted in the distance. 'It is in a woman's nature to strive to overcome her own failings, and the failings of her mother, and her mother before that, is it not? To seek adventure no matter what the cost, and to leave our manfolk behind to guard the adventuresses to come.'

'It is. Sometimes I wish I was born a man. Imagine, we could be within a home right now, safely ensconced, with no desire upon us to journey far.'

'We could,' Isabella agreed. 'It is a good life, for them, but I would not have my own journey otherwise.'

'And I agree.' Valentino looked out to sea, where the *Smiling Henry* had disappeared from view. 'Even though nobody will know our own story, and we will leave no little girls to bear our names, I am content. I am content to die

THE LAST VOYAGE OF THE SMILING HENRY

here, having seen more than I ever thought to see.'

'And so it ends. Shall we return to the cave?' asked
Isabella, and bowed to the first officer. Valentino returned
the gesture, and the two of them set off on a slow stroll up
to the one safe haven in an island of terror, enjoying the
sensations of being alive, strong, and courageous in an
unknown land.

ABOUT THE AUTHOR

Aliya Whiteley is the author of the novels *The Beauty, The Arrival of Missives, Skein Island, Light Reading, Three Things About Me, Mean Mode Median*, and a collection of short stories called *Witchcraft in the Harem*. She has had almost one hundred short stories published in various anthologies and publications including *The Guardian, Interzone, Black Static*, and *Strange Horizon*s. She has been nominated for the Pushcart Prize twice, and won the Drabblecast People's Choice Award. *The Arrival of Missives* has been shortlisted for the BSFA award for Best Short Fiction and longlisted for the James Tiptree Jr Award.

THE BEAUTY
Aliya Whiteley

Somewhere away from the cities and towns, in the Valley
of the Rocks, a society of men and boys gather around the
fire each night to listen to their history recounted by Nate,
the storyteller. Requested most often by the group is
the tale of the death of all women.

They are the last generation.

One night, Nate brings back new secrets from the woods;
peculiar mushrooms are growing from the ground where the
women's bodies lie buried. These are the first signs of a strange
and insidious presence unlike anything ever known before…

Discover the Beauty.

"Elegantly chilling, utterly heartbreaking horror."
M. R. Carey, author of *The Girl with All the Gifts*

"The brilliant gender-bending, post apocalyptic horror fable the
world needs right now. This book messed me up, in the best way
possible." Paul Tremblay, author of *A Head Full of Ghosts*

TITANBOOKS.COM

CLADE

James Bradley

On a beach in Antarctica, scientist Adam Leith marks the passage of the summer solstice. Back in Sydney his partner Ellie waits for the results of her latest round of IVF treatment.

That result, when it comes, will change both their lives and propel them into a future neither could have predicted.
In a collapsing England, Adam will battle to survive an apocalyptic storm. Against a backdrop of growing civil unrest at home, Ellie will discover a strange affinity with beekeeping. In the aftermath of a pandemic, a young man finds solace in building virtual recreations of the dead. And new connections will be formed from the most unlikely beginnings.

"A brilliant, unsettling and timely novel: a true text of the Anthropocene in its subtle shuttlings between lives, epochs and eras, and its knitting together of the planet's places."
Robert Macfarlane, author of *The Old Ways*

"Urgent, powerful stuff."
The Guardian

THE RIFT
Nina Allan

Selena and Julie are sisters. As children they were close, but as they grow older, a rift develops between them. There are greater rifts, however. Julie goes missing aged seventeen. It will be twenty years before Selena sees her again. When Julie reappears, she tells Selena an incredible story about how she has spent time on another planet. Does Selena dismiss her sister as a the victim of delusions, or believe her, and risk her own sanity?

"A heart-rending novel about being believed, being trusted, and the temptation to hide the truth... A generous book, it leaves the reader looking at the world anew. Dizzying stuff."
Anne Charnock, author of *Dreams Before the Start of Time*

"Beautifully told, absorbing, and eerie in the best way. I was left contemplating its images of alienation, connection, and parasitic threat days after I had finished reading it."
Yoon Ha Lee, author of *Ninefox Gambit*

THE RACE
Nina Allan

A child is kidnapped with consequences that extend across worlds... A writer reaches into the past to discover the truth about a possible murder... Far away a young woman prepares for her mysterious future...

The Race weaves together story threads and realities to take us on a gripping and spellbinding journey.

"Totally assured – this is a literate, intelligent, gorgeously human and superbly strange SF novel that will continually skewer your assumptions."
Alastair Reynolds, author of *Revenger*

"Every now and then, a debut novel knocks you blind... *The Race* will, as the best fiction should, have your compass spinning."
Strange Horizons

THE GRADUAL
Christopher Priest

Alesandro grows up in Glaund, a fascist state
constantly at war. His brother is drafted; his family
is destroyed by grief. He catches glimpses of islands
in the far distance from the shore, and they inspire
his music—music for which he is feted. His search for
his brother brings him into contact with the military
leadership and suddenly he is a fugitive on the run.
His endless travels take him through places and time,
bringing him answers he could not have forseen.

"Priest knows exactly what he is doing –
and is doing it brilliantly."
Chicago Tribune on *The Adjacent*

"Endlessly tantalizing and ultimately very
satisfying... Overall, rather stunning."
Locus on *The Adjacent*

For more fantastic fiction, author events, exclusive
excerpts, competitions, limited editions and more

VISIT OUR WEBSITE
titanbooks.com

LIKE US ON FACEBOOK
facebook.com/titanbooks

FOLLOW US ON TWITTER
@TitanBooks

EMAIL US
readerfeedback@titanemail.com